What Lies Behind Closed Doors.

By Sue Lacey

ISBN-13: 9781729369883

Acknowledgements for the cover for this
work go to Carli Hall, with grateful thanks for
her help and encouragement.

Also to Nathan Davey who first made me
believe it may be possible to publish it, and
Joshua Marshall for his technical assistance.

The characters and events in this book are
purely fictional

Table of Contents

Chapter one.

Cape Town 1944

The suggestion had been made on impulse but with genuine feeling behind it, but it had been firmly brushed away as a bad joke by Sarah.

"Mother, why not, you know it's what you both want in the end, and it would make our day perfect to share it with you as a double wedding. You can't go on turning George down forever. Besides, I don't want to go to England and leave you here in Cape Town alone."

Sarah Lawes and her daughter Lizzie had spent an exhausting morning sorting through twenty-one years' worth of personal belongings, clothes and memories in an attempt to decide what should go and what should stay. Lizzie had been brought up by her mother since her father died of a sudden heart attack at the age of only forty-five when she was ten years old. Except for the six months following his death, when Sarah had suffered such deep depression that she had been admitted to hospital and Lizzie put into a children's home, they had never been apart.

Lizzie never liked looking back on her time in the home as she had felt as if her young life had been torn apart, leaving her away from the comfort of her family, and in a totally alien environment where she never felt she could make friends with the other children and, although she supposed the staff there meant well, she too was grieving for her father and missing her mother terribly.

After some time Sarah had made a good recovery, retrieved her daughter, and vowed never to let anything or anyone come between them or hurt them again. However, the separation and uncertainty had also taken its toll on young Lizzie, and so the pair had spent a great deal of time rebuilding their relationship, meaning that Sarah had committed herself to her daughter with the exclusion of all others.

She had firmly turned down the suggestion from others to take in lodgers ("after all," they had said, "the house is too big for just the two of you"), instead choosing to sell up and move to a smaller bungalow on the road out of town. Lizzie would have preferred to remain in the old home in which she had grown up, but though they had been left reasonably well catered for financially, the house *was* too big for just two, and something inexplicable to Lizzie's mind about the idea of taking in lodgers, had convinced Sarah that she had no choice but to move. Expenses in their new home were subsidised by Sarah dressmaking and giving occasional piano lessons, which meant that their lives were actually quite comfortable and lacking very little. Even through the dark days of the Second World War their lives were not affected to any great extent. In fact, the war really had reasonably little effect on Cape Town save providing a base for the RAF base at nearby Brooklyn Airfield.

As a means of self-help and to prevent any chance of that terrible depression returning Sarah would often play the piano at the fortnightly tea dance held nearby, and it was at one of these that she had first made the acquaintance of George Gavenas. George was a round faced, jolly chap born of Anglo/Russian descent who worked as a jeweller. Whether it was because they were about the same age (her first husband, John Lawes, had been fourteen years her senior), because they both loved dancing, or just because he was so easy-going, Sarah had taken to him from the outset. Lizzie too had become very fond of George, not least for the calming affect he had on her mother. Though he was never allowed to stay in the house, George offered Lizzie much fatherly advice through the years that followed. It had been him who put forward the suggestion that Lizzie should join the staff on the nearby Royal Air Force base, and it was here that she had met the tall, handsome young Londoner, Harry Whiting who had swept her off her feet and proposed within four weeks of their meeting knowing full well that, with the war gradually coming to an end, he could be posted back to England at any time and couldn't bear the thought of losing her.

Sarah, of course, had taken a lot more convincing. Strangely suspicious of poor Harry's motives and his apparent eagerness to rush her daughter into this marriage, Sarah tried first to 'roar' at Harry like a lioness protecting her cub in an attempt to scare him away! Lizzie pleaded with her not to be so unwelcoming. Undeterred, Harry had persisted, convinced that a non-confrontational approach was the best. Suggesting that they should meet much of the time in her presence at home, and inviting her to escort them on outings, Harry proved his theory right and, with a word or two in the right place from George, persuaded Sarah that he was after all suitable husband material for her daughter.

On this particular day Lizzie sat beside her mother on the bed. They had always been very close, and yet Lizzie knew that, deep in her heart, there were things that mother had kept firmly locked away, things shared with no one, things that sometimes sent an unexplainable flash of fear through mother's eyes.

What these were Lizzie had no idea. Once before, when George suggested marriage to make the three of them a proper family, the expression on Sarah's face had not been wasted on her daughter. She saw that look of longing tinged with fear. Longing she could understand. Father had died nearly twelve years ago and Sarah had been 'keeping company' with George for four years now and her love for him was obvious. The tinge of fear was just for an instant, but clearly fear none the less. It had always been there in the background, woven like an invisible thread through their lives binding them together and keeping others out. All Lizzie knew was that it stemmed from her mother's early life in England but, until now, Sarah had kept it behind the closed doors of her mind.

It seemed to Lizzie that with the prospect of leaving her mother behind and travelling to England with Harry after the wedding, now might be the last opportunity to persuade her mother to unlock those closed doors. She had tried many times to suggest this, but the fear of unleashing the past had just caused Sarah to slam them closed each time. Lizzie felt it was different now, and so pursued the subject with more persistence than before and, to her surprise this persistence actually paid off this time.

"Perhaps now is the right time to explain Mother," she suggested gently. Sarah had known this day would come and could also see that time was slipping away.

"I suppose I do owe you an explanation, but to understand how and why I feel this way you really need to know the whole story, right from when I was young. You need to know about the lives of my parents, your grandparents. Only by knowing about them and what happened to us all will you appreciate and, well, hopefully understand, the consequences of what caused me to feel as I've felt all these years.

Reluctantly, almost fearfully, she heaved a sigh of resignation and began her story.

Chapter Two.

Birmingham, The early years

Taking her mind back into the distant and almost forgotten past, Sarah could hear her mother's voice calling through the cellar door.

"Come along you two. I really think it's time to take a break from whatever you're doing down there! Anyway, I think we are all in need of some fresh air, so I've packed a picnic lunch for us and thought we could go to the park as it's such a lovely day outside." Kate was determined to drag her family from the depths of the cellar before the day was out. This was one of Sarah's favourite memories from her childhood back in England so many years ago.

Kate was a quiet, gentle lady who had blossomed into a contented and confident wife since her marriage to Tom Burgess in June 1899, and even more so as a mother, since the birth of their daughter Sarah in September 1900, just over a year later.

Tom had worked hard to achieve his reputation as an extremely competent accountant in the hope of finding employment in a bank or business of some sort, as his father had done before him, but it had proved to take what seemed like so long to achieve this. Though he and Kate had been courting for a while he had been determined to be in a position to support her in a way he felt she deserved, and to provide her with a suitable home before going ahead with the wedding.

And now, after achieving his goal as a good and trustworthy employee as the bookkeeper in a local engineering company he felt free to marry Kate at last. Following the wedding the couple settled into a small, two bedroom terraced house, with hardly room to fit much furniture, but as they had very little this didn't worry Kate at all. The small box room was barely big enough to fit in a couple of shelves and small table, which Tom used as a desk, but this was fine for those first months until Sarah came along.

As was common in those days, Kate took a drawer from the dressing table in which to make a comfortable crib for her new born daughter and set it alongside their own bed so that she was within reach to nurse her baby when it became necessary. This arrangement suited them all at first, but it soon became apparent that Sarah would quickly outgrow her drawer, and need a room of her own, and that meant Tom having to give up his 'office' in the box room.

Still, he uttered not a word of complaint, just waited patiently each evening until Kate had cleared away the supper dishes and wiped off the table downstairs, before spreading his papers there to catch up with any outstanding work.

By the time she was ten years old, surrounded by the love that radiated from her parents young Sarah had grown into a pretty, intelligent young girl with a real sense of fun. It was around this time that the firm her father worked for closed down, leaving him unemployed.

Kate felt the first pangs of panic set in. Since their marriage, though they had not been wealthy by any means, they had always felt secure in the knowledge that a weekly pay packet was to be relied upon. She need not have worried. Tom had built up such a reputation as a capable and well respected member of the local community that two weeks later he came home with the news that he had been taken on as accountant for the firm of William Lawes & Son, a much larger and more prestigious engineering company to the one he had worked for previously. "What is more," he told his wife, "I shall be earning more money, and there is a house belonging to the company which I will be able to rent if you like it."

"Do you mean it, is it bigger than this one, can we afford it," Kate felt a real tingle of excitement running through her whole body. So many questions, so much to take in at once…

"Hang on dear, slow down with your questions. The main thing being that we'll have a home, a better home than this, and a good, secure job bringing in a wage good enough, not to make us rich, but to guarantee our Sarah a good start in life."

The next morning the Burgess family were up, washed and dressed with surprising speed. The agent working for the Lawes Company was to meet them at the house in question so that they might have a viewing of it to decide on its suitability, although in Kate's eyes this was a forgone conclusion. Both her and their young daughter had already decided that it had to be a step up from their present home if it had any more space in it. From Tom's point of view it would certainly be so much more convenient to be that much closer to his new place of work.

A short tram ride took the family to within walking distance of the new house and, on turning the corner of the street, the agent was there awaiting their arrival.

Kate managed to keep her excitement under control as she felt appropriate for the wife of someone in Tom's position, whilst Sarah obediently followed her parents around the house, secretly working out which would be her room, and how she would arrange her meagre belongings in it.

The matter was soon settled and within the week Tom had found a friend with a small van to help move their belongings into their new abode. Though this took rather more than one journey it allowed Kate and her daughter the time to shuffle things around, deciding on the best places for everything between loads. By the time all the furniture was in place Kate had lit the stove, found the kettle, and made a much needed pot of tea to help down the slices of rich fruit cake she had prepared in advance for them all.

Chapter Three

Settling in.

The new house was a moderately substantial three bedroom end terrace property sitting in the suburbs of Birmingham. Though owned by his employer, Tom still had a quite substantial rent to pay but, taking into account the increased income he received from the new position he now held with the company, they were determined to manage it.

On the practical side, Kate pointed out, they did now have a spare room, and were therefore in a position to take in a lodger to help with the expense. At first Tom was not at all happy with the idea of allowing a stranger to share their home with them, but Kate being the practical lady that she was, soon reasoned with him to at least give it a try.

Accordingly Tom checked with his new employer the next day that taking in a lodger would be acceptable and was told that, as long as it was just one, and a respectable one at that, Mr Lawes had no objections to the idea. An advert was duly displayed in the window of the local post office offering 'a single room accommodation for one occupant, possible with breakfast and an evening meal provided for the right person.'

Kate figured that, as she would be preparing meals for her family, one extra mouth to feed would make little difference. She was convinced that this arrangement would work extremely satisfactorily. The first person to approach them in connection with this was a lady by the name of Mrs Hackett who was looking for lodgings in the area for her thirteen year old daughter, Ann. In desperation to avoid either working in service or in a factory, Ann had managed to secure a position as an apprentice dressmaker at a shop in town, and her mother was keen to find a respectable place for her to stay.

It seemed from what she told Kate that Ann was the eldest of five children in a family of two boys and three girls. Mrs Hackett's first husband had passed away just three years after Ann was born, but she had remarried some two years later, meaning that her other four children were considerably younger than Ann. With this age gap, it was therefore not surprising that she had been brought up to help her Mother making clothes for her younger siblings, standing her in good stead to take on this new role.

Annie, as she was known, soon became close friends with young Sarah, in spite of the three year age difference, and whilst she acted in many ways as an older sister for Sarah, Kate in turn took her under her wing almost as an older daughter. Tom had to admit that this arrangement had proved to be satisfactory all round and, though only a pittance towards the rent, the little extra made the difference between struggling and managing with something near to comfort.

His first month in the new employment also proved most satisfactory. He was given a small office to himself in which to work, and soon proved himself extremely capable and trustworthy to Mr Lawes snr.

A while into his employment Tom enquired of the foreman who and where was the '& son'. Perhaps, he thought, this referred to William and his father; or was William's son too young to join the company yet?

"No," said the foreman, "It's quite sad really, but the old man lost his wife when the boy was small and seems to have done his level best to ignore him since. Packed him off to boarding school as soon as he could. Think he's out in Africa somewhere now, supposed to be setting up a branch out there making tracks for engines."

"That's a great shame, I really can't imagine how much you must hurt to turn your back on your own son like that." Tom shuddered at the thought of how terrible it would be to lose Kate, but even so couldn't for one minute begin to imagine turning his back on his beloved Sarah, even under such dire circumstances. He had remembered his own parents explaining that they had tragically lost a daughter the year before he was born, meaning he'd lost a sister, a thing which always regretted, yet they had never allowed it to retract from their affection for him. The doctors had thought it unlikely his mother would be able to produce any more children, but she had proved them wrong when Tom had arrived safely and survived. They had made the decision at that point to count their blessing and be content with the child they had been blessed with.

After the Burgess family had occupied the house for about a month they began to acquire a few new (or good second-hand) items of furniture, meaning that there was now room for both family members and lodger to sit comfortably, giving Kate space to sit and either crochet, knit or sometimes read if she had found time to visit the library in Birmingham.

Young Sarah and her friend and 'pretend' big sister Annie would enjoy playing board games, an occupation which suited Sarah as she was always wanting to stretch her brain power, but still found times when she enjoyed Annie teaching her the basics of simple needlework, though she soon found she didn't share quite the skills in this occupation as her friend.

Sometimes the two girls would help Kate in the kitchen where she taught them useful culinary skills which meant that, not only did they pick up useful tips, but she had more time to do other necessary work around the house, or pop out to do shopping, or call in for a quiet cup of tea and a chat with May Jackson from next door.

In the time the Burgess family had lived there they had found the neighbours to be quite friendly towards them, and particularly in the case of the Jacksons' who lived next door. Bill had been more than willing to help Tom unload the furniture from the van into the house the day they moved in, and May had been such a help that day giving Kate a hand putting up curtains and making up beds. She was also quick to invite them all round for hot drinks and a proper meal later that day, knowing it would take a while to sort out the kitchen sufficiently to prepare anything. Since that day Kate and May remained close friends.

As time went on the two girls grew ever closer. When Kate was busy Annie was always more than happy to take Sarah out around town or sometimes to visit Annie's family.

Sarah took to Annie's mother from the start as she was such a warm and welcoming sort of person, but still it was clear to see that the younger four children were quite a handful for her to cope with.

There was Sam, the eldest boy, who was about six years younger than Annie, which made him around three years younger than Sarah. Heading on for seven years old he was already beginning to think of himself as being of an age to make his own decisions, even those his mother told him not to! Then there was Susie, a pretty, gentle natured five year old, who seemed permanently intent on seeking attention from either her mother, or from big sister Annie. This she would demand, pushing her way in whenever mother spent any time attending to the many needs of the three year old twins, Mary and Luke.

The Hackett home was certainly never dull, no more was it ever quiet. It seemed to Sarah that poor Mrs Hackett never had a minute to herself, though she was never heard to complain.

Although never looking completely in control of her offspring, it seemed that the thing that had most effect on their behaviour was the regularly heard phrase, "if you don't behave I'll be telling your father when he gets home." To Sarah's amusement this always had an immediate effect.

Annie explained that her mother often had trouble coping due to her ongoing health problems, probably exacerbated by bringing five children into the world, and the fact that she was now on the verge of producing another!

Sarah couldn't help thinking that it wasn't so bad being an only child after all.

Back at home it soon became clear to poor Tom that the three females seemed to be monopolising most of the space. When, as he did from time to time, he brought some of his accounts home to do away from the noise and dust of the factory, he found himself confined to doing this on a tray on his lap, or when it was not in use, on the kitchen table!

One Saturday morning when Annie had to work, the Burgess family decided not to waste what had turned out to be a really lovely sunny Saturday morning. Tom, Kate and Sarah were strolling towards the park when Kate happened to glance into the window of old Mr Wilson's second hand furniture shop when she stopped dead in her tracks and exclaimed,

"Look Tom, that's just what you need."

He stopped and turned round to see what had caught her eye. There just inside the door was a large, leather topped desk in absolutely beautiful condition.

"I doubt we can afford that dear," he told her, but old Mr Wilson had already overheard the conversation and was heading towards them.

"Good morning to you Mr and Mrs Burgess, and young Sarah. My, how you have grown my dear. How old are you now?"

"I'll be eleven in two weeks' time Mr Wilson," Sarah told him proudly.

Determined not to miss a chance of a sale the old man was more than happy to negotiate a very reasonable price, even going to the lengths of stating that he would get his boys to carry it to the house that very afternoon.

And so the deal was done and the desk duly delivered at three o'clock sharp that very afternoon as promised.

There just remained one major problem … where to put it! In all her enthusiasm to make life as comfortable for her dear Tom as possible, Kate had not taken into account just how big the desk would look squashed into a corner of the front room.

Never mind, she thought, we will manage somehow. It was too good a bargain to be missed. In the end some weeks later it was Sarah who came up with an unexpected solution to the problem.

The hallway coming in from the front door was quite long and narrow with dado rails along the length of it, and two doors opening to the left. The first door led into the front room, and the second led into the kitchen. Outside, beyond the kitchen, was an old, and rather neglected scullery. It seemed this had hardly been altered for many years, except for the obvious addition of a fairly new concrete floor, probably to repair damage to the existing one. Now Mother used this space in which to do her laundry in the copper which stood in the corner, before hanging it out on the line to dry in the back yard.

On the right side of the hall there was the stairs leading up to the bedrooms above. Here there were two rooms; one at the front of the house where Tom and Kate slept, and one at the back which was Sarah's. Another small staircase led up to the attic room which was the one let out to Annie. Though originally servant's quarters, this was a substantial sized room.

One day as Sarah was standing near the kitchen doorway speaking to her Mother her fingers traced idly along the dado, past the kitchen door, into the corner of the wall, and on along the apparent end wall of the hall. She couldn't help noticing the difference in level of the rail, and the fact that this wall had a hollow sound to it when she tapped it.

"Do you know," she said, "I don't believe this is a solid wall like the others. Do you think it's been covered up for some reason Mother?"

"I suppose it's possible, but I can't imagine why, or what would be behind it, unless it was another door into the back yard." Kate came and gave it a tap just the same.

By the time Father had arrived home from work that night all three female members of the household were full of speculation and curiosity as to what lay hidden behind the false wall.

An escape route; but who for and from whom? Perhaps a second servant's staircase from the attic to the kitchen? But there wasn't any sign or room for this at the back of the house. Then of course there was Sarah's favourite idea, one that only someone with such a vivid imagination as her could dream up.

"Perhaps some poor soul was walled up alive between the outside wall and the false one!"

It was pointless Tom attempting to reason with them all. There was nothing left but to try to remove, as carefully as possible, the false wall to solve the mystery and satisfy them all.

To do this he would need tools. Being purely brilliant with his mind but absolutely useless with his hands, this was something he simply didn't possess. Luckily by now he felt sufficiently acquainted with Bill from next door, a man with the exactly opposite abilities to Tom, to ask for a loan of the tools necessary to do the job.

An hour and much encouragement later Tom managed to strip off the dado rail, then with even more effort and encouragement, prise away what seemed to be just one large board across the wall. To everyone's astonishment this revealed an old door. Unlike the other doors in the hall, this was not a panelled door, but just a plain boarded door with a latch rather than a knob as the others had.

"You see," exclaimed Sarah, "I bet someone was locked behind that door."

As soon as she said it Sarah began to wish she'd not had such an awful thought. For a few minutes they all stood looking at the door as though half expecting someone to open it.

Chapter Four

The cellar & family life.

After the initial surprise had worn off Tom stepped forward to open the door. At first this proved particularly difficult as, obviously, it hadn't been opened for many years. The lift-up latch was pretty rusty and badly in need of replacing, so much so that, when the door finally did open, the inside latch broke off.

"Never mind, I expect I can fix it one day," Tom remarked.

Peering in through the door it appeared to Tom and Kate that there seemed to be steps going down. Kate ran back along the hall and fetched a gas lamp from the hall table to enable her husband to investigate further. Within a few minutes he appeared back up the stairs and through the door with news that below here there was quite a substantial cellar.

"It'll need a good clear out, but I think it'll solve the problem of where to put my desk, and it will certainly be a quiet place to work away from chattering females!" he said with a laugh.

He was certainly right about the need for a good clear out down there, but the next day being a Saturday, everybody set to, removing rubbish, dislodging cobwebs and sweeping the floor. By later that day Tom's new 'office' was ready for use.

When he took Bill's tool box back that afternoon, it seemed that Bill had never heard of any of these houses having cellars, "But then I've not been here so long either, so perhaps just never looked."

Bill was only too pleased to oblige by helping Tom carry the desk along the hall and, with all the effort they could muster, manoeuvre it carefully down the stairs into the cellar, or what Sarah declared was now her father's office.

"If you want some help putting up shelves just let me know. I've got quite a lot of planks stacked away in my shed I could do with getting rid of mate."

"Sounds like a good idea, as long as you really don't need them," Tom was already working out in his head how best to make best use of these.

With a little help again from his kind neighbour the promised rows of shelves were soon put up along one wall to hold any files or books Tom might choose to keep handy, and last but not least, Kate allotted him a good strong chair on which to sit whilst at his desk.

Tom was thrilled to have a space to himself, away from the chatter of the female members of the household, and declared this to be strictly out of bounds for anything other than his work and certainly of anything that might distract him from it!

As he had already proved himself to be a reliable and conscientious book keeper, Mr Lawes was prepared to allow him to bring a certain amount of paperwork home to do, agreeing that the office he'd been allotted at the factory was extremely noisy most of the time. Also, once he was up to date with the work for the company, he sometimes was able to take on the odd piece of work for a couple of much smaller firms locally.

Once established in his cellar office, Tom would retreat into its depths and loose himself in his work, but as the devoted family man that he was, he always found time to share with 'his girls', as he referred to them. Any spare time he had when the weather was fine he would enjoy nothing better than a stroll through the park or along by the canal, but when he had much to do by way of work he was adamant that no disturbances would be brooked.

Even so, from an early age young Sarah had grown up happy to be 'Daddies girl' and dogged his every footstep, often even into the cellar where usually entry was forbidden! As she grew up and began to show a keen interest in the work he was doing Father gradually relented and allowed her to follow him down there, but only on condition that she sat quietly by his side and learnt a little of budgeting and basic bookkeeping. In fact, by the time she was nearly twelve years old, Tom was really quite amazed at how much she had learnt.

"I can see that she must be well above a lot of her class at school. She seems to take in all that I'm doing with such ease," he told his wife.

Because of this they would stay in their own little soundproof world for hours at a time until Kate chose to drag them to the surface for the occasional meal, or to join her for that much needed walk or a picnic in the park. For all Kate scolded them for this, she really was pleased to watch the closeness which was so unmistakeable between father and daughter, and both made it clear that this same closeness very much included her.

In much later years, adult Sarah looked back to these times and smiled to herself as she remembered with amusement how Father, with his tendency to be rather more of a business man than a handyman, was rather inclined to let certain things slip by unattended. There was always the 'small' matter of the latch on the inside of the cellar door which had been broken off as they had prised the door open for the first time, leaving the 'temporary' repair of a length of string to prevent the outer latch from dropping, thereby making it impossible to open the door from inside. If the outside latch was not hooked up firmly this would drop as the door slammed closed, imprisoning them until rescue came from outside! This happened on frequent occasions and, after suitable admonishment from Mother, was always followed by a promise from Father to make the necessary adjustments 'immediately'. The nearest this promise came to reality though was a fresh loop of string after the first one became worn to prevent the offending latch from dropping....as long as someone remembered to use it! But usually both were so engrossed in what they were doing that neither noticed their mistake until rescued and firmly reprimanded by Kate.

Life was good then. They were a happy family.

All this was to change with the coming of outbreak of WW1 in 1914. For some months Sarah had heard the men, including her Father and Bill the neighbour, talking about the unrest going on across Europe.

Having left school as she reached the end of her twelfth year, partly due to her Father's influence and encouragement with the time spent in his office, Sarah had been lucky enough to find employment in a basic secretarial capacity for one of the smaller companies he did occasional work for and had been there for some months. She was soon aware of the same subject of conversation gradually wafting across the staff room like smoke through a forest.

Though she considered herself to be quite bright and quick to learn most things, Sarah found world politics went way over her head. From what she could understand there seemed to be treaties between groups of countries, meaning that they had agreed to stand together should another declare war on one of them.

Father tried to explain that Germany was in alignment with Austria-Hungary. "So are we with them too," she asked.

"No dear," Tom tried to explain, "We have a similar treaty with Ireland, France and Russia, try not to worry yourself about it dear, it won't affect us."

But Tom, as was the case with most men at that point, was watching the news with growing trepidation. On 28th June that year came the assassination of Archduke Franz Ferdinand in Sarajevo. The chain of events following on from this became so rapid that it seemed so unreal. Austria-Hungary and Germany threatened war on Serbia, while Russia sided with the Serbians.

It became clear that Europe was on the brink of war. By August 1st Germany declared war on Russia, followed swiftly by declaring war on France on August 3rd. The following day, August 4th, German troops marched into Belgium on route to France.

Back in Britain those in authority had been watching this unfold and, as this country had agreed to be in alliance with these countries to help maintain their neutrality, were already prepared to come to their defence. Sir Edward Grey, Britain's foreign secretary, had given Germany an ultimatum to withdraw, but this did not happen, and so, as those gathered round their radios to listen, he was heard to announce that 'consequently this country is at war with Germany'.

Chapter Five

No turning back.

Shortly after declaring war on Germany, posters were going up everywhere with the face of Field-Marshall Lord Kitchener and his finger pointing out and saying, 'Your country needs you.' Another pasted up on the post office window gave the message, 'Women of Britain say – GO!' encouraging them to push their menfolk to sign up and show willing to fight for King and country.

This was going on all over the country, and there seemed no shortage of volunteers, all believing in the cause of the defence of the European countries, and therefore preventing the threat to our own. The poster that Sarah was most concerned about was on a wall outside the tram station every morning on her way to work. She couldn't help but see it whilst waiting with Annie a few days later. This one showed a long snake-like column of men, civilians, with the message, 'Step into your place', written across the top.

"Father won't go though will he," she asked her Mother anxiously that evening. Surely he wouldn't have to go and leave his girls for a war that everyone was saying wouldn't last long. It all seemed rather silly to her and too distant to involve everybody. Though Kate desperately wanted to reassure her daughter on this score she could not lie to her. All she could bring herself to say was, "Let's just pray it won't come to that dear."

Sitting on the bed in Annie's room later that evening, Annie too had to admit that she too was worried about just how all this would affect her family. By now her mother had given birth to a robust baby boy who she named Matthew. Though this was a month ago now, the strain of delivering this rather large baby at her age had taken its toll on her health, leaving her in a more delicate state than before.

"Mum will never manage if Dad has to go," and then, realising she must not scare Sarah unnecessarily, "But we mustn't panic, fingers crossed our Dad's will stay at home. They surely can't all go."

Kate tried hard to persuade Tom not to join up but, as with so many of his generation, it seemed the right thing to do to defend the country at all costs and fight for the King. Without warning he returned home from work later than usual one day and broke the news that he had signed up for the Royal Warwickshire Battalion and would shortly be receiving call up papers to advise him as to where to report for training.

Kate was quite naturally distressed at the prospect of her beloved Tom, that gentlest of men, being sent to fight, let alone kill, but managed to put on a false air of acceptance as a means of reassurance to Sarah.

On the day before Sarah's fourteenth birthday the dreaded call up papers arrived. In fact it seemed that practically all the men in the street also received theirs that same day. It seemed to the wives and families that their husbands, fathers and sons were all to be whisked away from them at once with frightening speed, leaving them no time to prepare for their loss.

At first Sarah felt a mixture of pride in her father for volunteering, but this was quickly overtaken by fear at the thought of him becoming one of the unrecognisable column she had seen on the poster at the tram stop. As with so many at that stage, she did not fully realise the impact this could have on their family, yet she knew that life would never be quite the same without him.

Not until the day came for him to depart did the full reality of his actions hit home. Tom wrapped his arms around his daughter and told her how proud he was of her, how much he loved her, and how he knew she would look after Mother till he returned. Then he turned to Kate, at which point she could hold back the tears no longer and neither could he. Hardly a word passed between them... words were not needed. A last kiss, a last fond embrace, and he was gone off down the street with barely a glance behind him.

Chapter Six

Struggle to cope.

Without the means of communication we are used to in our modern times, even those available during WW2, Kate knew little of what and where Tom's regiment was. None the less she kept up writing to him regularly in the hope that her letters, along with her love, were finding their way to him somehow. For a while just after he left she did receive the odd letter card from him, but these were limited as to what they were allowed to say, and seldom gave much comfort except in knowing he was at least still alive.

This of course applied to all families with menfolk away fighting. Nobody really expected to read reports in the newspapers of such unbelievable slaughter during those early months. It seemed that right across France and Belgium all that was achieved was sheer carnage, usually on both sides. As if the fighting in this part of Europe was not sufficient, it had by this time spread across so many countries that it seemed to consume the world.

Still, many had said at the start that the war 'would be over by Christmas', a hope encouraged as there were now reports in those same papers of how the guns had gone silent on Christmas morning along the Western Front, the first silence since it had begun. It was said that the troops on both sides had called a truce and come up out of their trenches to swap cigarettes, sweets, handkerchiefs and the like, sing carols, and that they had even participated in a game of football together! They had also taken the opportunity to recover and bury their dead comrades.

Surely, the families back home had hoped, this must be a good sign, a sign that they may decide to come to some sort of compromise. Unfortunately this was not the case as the Christmas truce lasted just for that morning, but come the afternoon the ceasefire gave way and the killing resumed.

Kate, as did many in her situation, began to worry about the gradual drop in their finances. Although she received money from Tom's pay, she was finding that this was actually less than he had been bringing home before the war. Of course there was Sarah's weekly contribution to their living expenses, but this only helped to a certain degree.

This was made so much harder by the loss of Annie's rent. Within a week after Tom leaving Annie had visited her mother to find that, without her husband there to help her, she was just finding it all too much to cope with alone. Consequently Annie, feeling she was really left with no choice, had reluctantly made the decision to move back home to help her take care of the children and run the house, while at the same time having to find part time work to support them all.

Bearing in mind the fact that this little extra from their lodger's rent had made such a difference in the first place, this drop in Kate's income now meant mother and daughter having to watch every penny even more closely, and gave Kate increasing cause for concern.

During the early months of 1915 she decided to look for assorted part-time employment wherever it became available, but this still seemed rather a paltry amount. Being so many women in the same situation, many not even having been left in anything like as good a situation as Kate, she found she was just one of many after the few available jobs. Still, being the practical and resourceful person she was, she did her very best to make the best of whatever she could find.

On her way home from the shop on the corner one day Kate met May Jackson from next door also heading homeward.

"Would you care for a cuppa May," she asked, "I'm just going to put the kettle on."

Since the men had left the two had become good friends and would often pop in for tea and a chat. Although Kate had Sarah when she wasn't at work, May and Bill's children had long since left home, and this meant that now she was particularly thankful for her neighbours company from time to time.

"I'm thinking of advertising for a temporary lodger again," Kate told May, "but I don't really know if I'm too sure of having a stranger move in while there's no man in the house. I know we had young Annie, but that was different, and Tom was here too then. It'd be different taking in an older person, let alone a man."

Reluctant as Kate was, her practical side kicked in and so she put an advert in the local shop window and set too preparing the spare room in the hope of finding a lodger to occupy it, preferably hoping this might be a someone of a respectable nature, and someone both she and Sarah could feel at ease with enough to share their home.

It seemed it was a case of first time lucky on both counts. A few days later Kate and Sarah were sitting at the table contemplating taking the dishes to the kitchen to wash up when the doorbell rang. Sarah rushed the dirty crockery out of sight while her mother, after a quick check in the hall mirror, went to answer the door.

"Good afternoon Madam, I believe you may have a room available," enquired a tall, dark haired gentleman Kate estimated to be between twenty-five and thirty years old. Kate was pleasantly surprised as she could see immediately by his manner and appearance that this was a gentleman of substantial breeding, and thankfully not the type she was dreading coming to her door. Perhaps, she thought, this might not work out as badly as she had feared.

"Allow me to introduce myself. My name is Lawes, John Lawes. I am led to believe that your husband is known to my father, Mr William Lawes, through his work."

Recognition came over Kate's countenance as she heard the name. Yes, Tom had been employed for some time by William Lawes to attend to his accounts before going off to war. She knew him to be a good and generous man, always quick to pay Tom what was owed, unlike some he had worked for in the past, and it had been him taking the job with Lawes and Son company which had given him the opportunity to take the house they now occupied.

"Oh yes, please come in Mr Lawes. Allow me to show you the room," a very relieved Kate offered. "I'm afraid it isn't particularly large, but I believe it to be reasonably comfortable. The bed is almost new and I believe there is adequate furniture to hold sufficient clothing and the like."

Mr Lawes followed her through the hall and up the stairs where, having seen it, he assured Kate that he was more than satisfied with the room. "Yes, thank you Mrs Burgess, I believe the room will suit me admirably."

Kate escorted him downstairs and introduced him to Sarah who had taken it upon herself to make some tea for them to drink, pouring three cups while Kate explained the circumstances that had led her to let the room. She added that she would be happy to provide an evening meal for Mr Lawes on his return from work each day. In fact, though she didn't say as much, she felt it would be so good to have a man to cook for as she had always done for Tom. Somehow, in spite of having her dear daughter for company, the house had felt so empty without a male presence since he had been gone, and somehow she felt a genuine sense of comfort knowing she'd found one she could feel safe around.

Feeling the need to make a better explanation as to just how and why he came to be needing lodgings, John explained to them that he had come to the area to work with his father to get to know and eventually take over the business. In spite of his reasonably young age it seemed that he had been abroad for a few years, during which time he had been both married, then widowed, within a year. Sadly, it seemed his wife had died at quite an early age, giving birth to their child. Both mother and child having died had obviously been an extremely painful experience, one on which Kate knew better than to question him further.

Now he had returned as his father, due to failing health, was finding the running of the business rather too much to cope with alone. He would only need accommodation for a matter of weeks though as the plan was to find himself a house.

Although Kate didn't like to ask, she did think it strange that he seemed not to have any intention of moving into his father's house. Of course Tom had not mentioned the conversation he'd had about the Lawes family when he first went to work there. She assumed he must have his reasons, after all the house William Lawes lived in was spacious enough for a lot more than one elderly gentleman and a couple of staff. This much she already knew from having a more than passing acquaintance with Mrs. Betts, Mr Lawes cook, and of course, friend or no friend, Mrs Betts was too loyal to discuss her employer's private business behind his back. Never mind, whatever the reason she felt somehow that his presence in this house would be more than welcome.

An agreement was quickly reached regarding rent, tea was drunk, and John Lawes took his leave of them. The next day he returned complete with a trunk full of belongings, suitably covered in stickers which, when seeing this in the hall as she came home that evening, Sarah found intriguing. Obviously these were proof, if proof was needed, of his recent travels, the most recent of which seemed to be South Africa where, sometime later, he explained he had been considering returning to further his business interests if his father agreed to his plans.

Chapter Seven

The Lodger

John Lawes proved to be a quiet and considerate lodger. Once unpacked Kate suggested that, to make more space, he should store his empty trunk in the cellar. As she showed him this, she also said he was welcome to use Tom's desk should he have need of writing space, but with a firm warning not to close the door completely without putting the string in position as a means to prevent his entrapment! The tale of the finding, and the lack of repair on the door, seemed to greatly amuse him, but he promised to heed her warning.

"I'm afraid I'm not much of a handyman either," He said with a laugh in his voice, "but I'll perhaps see what I can do one day."

John left punctually at seven each morning and returned for his evening meal around six thirty each evening. Young Sarah always felt a little in awe of this slightly aloof gentleman, but felt, as did her mother, that there was something comforting about having the presence of a man in the house. As for John this arrangement also appeared to suit him well enough too, and so he chose to remain there and put his efforts into tackling the business rather than wasting time house hunting.

The business that William Lawes had built up over many years was an engineering company on the outskirts of Birmingham. John had been well versed in the organisation and running of this since a boy and so, at the age of twenty-four, had taken on the task of helping establish a branch of a similar company in South Africa where there was a great need for construction of railways etc. Indeed it had only been the threat of the upcoming war, added to his father's gradually declining health, which had persuaded him to return to England almost four years later.

Though great numbers were recruited into the forces sent from South Africa to fight for the British when war broke out, John Lawes was not amongst them. John had intended joining up along with his contemporaries but found that his skills were needed more in his father's engineering works as this had become a reserved occupation due to the factory being pressed into service to produce armaments and ammunition for the forces. This change was made worse by his father becoming less able to cope alone in his present state of health. Though he felt rather uncomfortable about being, as he saw it, safely ensconced at home whilst others were out there putting their lives on the line for their country, he had to accept the fact that they could certainly not do so without the weapons produced by factories such as his and others like it.

All this he explained to Kate and Sarah as they sat one evening after dinner. Sensing from their discussions over those early weeks, and knowing how badly they missed Tom, he felt an explanation was needed to prove to them that he was certainly not a coward, and that he would most definitely have gone had his father been able to cope without him. In fact it appeared that without him taking over the majority of the hard work of running the firm, it would be unable to take on the extra war work and would be forced to close.

Kate could sense a slight feeling of resentment behind that implication. It was obvious to her that he carried with him a genuine feeling of guilt. She found herself trying to reassure him that he was following the only course of action, one which supported the country in its own way, yet there was also on her part something ironic about them sitting in front of a cosy fireplace, discussing John's need to be making arms for her beloved Tom to be out there, wherever there was, using such weapons to kill or, more importantly, to keep from being killed!

That night Kate prayed extra hard.

Chapter Eight

Manchester 1916

Meanwhile the same had been happening in all parts of the country. Since the beginning of the war in 1914 men had felt the need to answer the call to arms through loyalty to their country. From the first call to arms men had been leaving in their droves, leaving parents, wives and children to cope without them, and certainly for the first months, without realising the full horror of what they were to face.

Even so, by 1915 numbers of volunteers were dropping drastically. To make up for the shortfall, in January the following year the Military Service Act 1916 was passed to introduce conscription for men aged eighteen to forty years old.

It was possible to appeal this on some grounds. Most who did were doing so on grounds of health or the fact that they were doing important war work. Others did so on moral or religious grounds, and were called conscientious objectors. Many of these were allowed to fill non-combatant duties as medical orderlies with the Royal Army Medical Corps or drivers. Those not agreeing to such roles were imprisoned, some even given a death sentence, and certainly reviled by the majority of the population as cowards.

Some were in fact genuinely keen to serve in whatever way possible but, due to really drastic circumstances, were unable to do so except by carrying out occasional local work freed up by the shortage of others.

Such a man was one by the name of Jack Sheppard. He had spent most of his working life in the mines. It was hard, dirty work, but he never complained as it brought in a good wage, or at least good enough to enable him to marry and provide a home for his childhood sweetheart, Mary. They had been together for six years and had been keen to start a family, but somehow this was not happening. Mary had been pregnant twice but miscarried on both occasions. Just as the war broke out it seemed their luck had changed. Mary produced a baby boy, small but apparently healthy.

But tragedy struck without warning a week after the birth when Jack came home from work to find his beloved Mary lying dead in their bed in a pool of blood, and his young son dead alongside her. The doctor explained that she had haemorrhaged badly, and that young Jack (to be named after his father), had had little chance anyway of surviving without his mother's milk so early.

Jack was absolutely devastated by the loss of both wife and son. To him it felt his world had come to an abrupt end. He had immediately took himself off to the recruiting post, figuring he would rather die for his country than live without his family.

Yet even this solution was not destined to work out for Jack. Due to the terrible state of his lungs from the constant exposure to coal dust he failed the medical miserably. He tried pleading with the doctors to let him go, saying he was happy to take his chances and was not concerned what risk he was taking, but to no avail, there was no way they would allow it. To Jack, bearing in mind the hundreds of young, healthy men dying there on the front, surely it wouldn't matter so much if he could be there and, perhaps, be killed in place of one of those with a life to come home to.

He had had to face the prospect of being unable to continue with the occupation he knew, losing his beloved wife and child, and now, just to make things so much more unbearable if that was at all possible, be made to feel of no use to king and country.

He could bear it no longer being in the same place, seeing the same faces of people he had known for most of his life. Within a couple of weeks of being rejected by the military Jack packed his belongings and left Newcastle. After roaming aimlessly for some time he found himself in Manchester.

Managing to acquire a few hours a week working in the nearby docks, he soon found himself able to rent two rooms in a rather dilapidated house just outside of town. It was not much of a home, rather bleak and bare, but Jack was past caring about comfort, just content to have an address without which he would be unable to find employment. This should have been sufficient at least to allow him to eat, but more often than not he felt so depressed that the pittance earnt was spent in one of the many pubs within walking distance.

Though he would drink alongside others local to the area, he very much kept himself to himself, never wanting to get to know anyone too closely, and ashamed to let them get to know the failure he had become.

Whilst Jack Sheppard was hiding away from his misery and the shame of being of no use to his country, there were others who had no shame and would use any available avoidance tactics to escape conscription.

One such man choosing to try these was a travelling salesman by the name of Sydney Hanson. A man of extremely dubious character, he had managed to slip by unnoticed so far by keeping on the move. Now, with conscription coming into play, this was not so easy. He tried every trick he could think of to find a way out of the armed forces, including feigning assorted medical conditions, but the army medical board were having none of it. His only solution therefore was to give up his job and, without means of support, just keep moving and keep his head down to avoid the authorities catching up with him.

By the time he found himself in Manchester he figured it would be reasonably safe to stop for a while, seeing as it was a busy and bustling place, even with the majority of fighting age men away, and therefore easier to blend in with what was remaining of the local population. He had really not intended staying in this area for too long, hoping that he could find a place to go, and some way to disappear from the authorities' long term. The problem with this plan was that he needed money to support himself which meant finding employment and this would of course require identifying paperwork, which in turn would scupper his objective of avoiding military service.

This was a man who was given to spending much of his time propping up bars and gambling, both of which more often than not led him into arguments and all out brawls with those around him, and here in Manchester proved to be no exception.

During one of his heavy drinking sessions he made the acquaintance of a local man by the name of Jack Sheppard. When Jack queried why Syd had not been called up, Syd, sounding surprisingly convincing, stuck to his chosen story, that he was unfit but didn't go into any great detail save to express his great sadness at being unable to fight for his country!

On hearing this Jack sighed and offered his sympathy, believing that Syd like him would really like to have joined up. He then tried to offer comfort by explaining that he too was in a similar position, explaining to Syd how his many years spent working in the coal mines meant that he'd suffered badly from respiratory problems. With his lungs shot to pieces as they were he had no chance of being accepted in any of the forces.

"I did apply for the army but was turned down, it leaves you feeling a bit useless doesn't it?" he said with a true air of sadness that most men would have understood, but not so Sydney Hanson. "When the paper came through to say I'd been turned down it came as quite a blow; makes you feel guilty when so many are putting their lives on the line and all you can do is stand here drowning your sorrows," Jack added.

At this snippet of information Hanson's ears pricked. A paper to say they'd turned him down... that's just what he needed. But as far as he could see there was no way to get hold of one, let alone one with his name on. This was a problem his beer soaked mind was in no state to work out just now but he knew it was something he needed to work on. Perhaps he should cultivate an acquaintance with this fool, he decided, there might be a solution when he was sober enough to give it some thought. For now all he wanted was a place to put his head down for the night as he'd been kicked out of his last place for abusing the landlord and not paying his rent.

"Don't worry about that mate," said Jack on hearing of Hanson's homelessness, "I've got a couple of rooms not far from here, and you're welcome to bunk down on the sofa for a few nights if you don't mind roughing it."

One less problem thought Syd, especially as this would probably mean he'd get food included if he played the hard up card right. Obviously, after all he decided, this Sheppard bloke was not the brightest, in fact was probably the softest touch he'd come across for ages!

Jack was right when he'd told Syd that his place was no palace, actually it was a bit of a dump, but it provided shelter for them both between drinking sessions. Jack explained to Hanson about his misfortune at losing his wife and son, and how he had been unable to continue to work at his previous employment, going on to relate his disappointment at being refused the chance even to volunteer for the forces, all of which Hanson could see just added to his depression.

There were a couple of photos of Mary on the walls, a thing that made Hanson feel even more a sense of how badly life had treated him. Though he had 'hung around' with assorted women over the years, he had little respect for their gender and therefore had never actually found one he could say would have agreed to marriage with him, even had it occurred to him to ask them. Syd could see that his new 'mate' probably only drank to help him cope with his situation, his loss and his rejection, whereas for him it was exactly the opposite reason; his way to avoid the truth that he may well not be able to escape the call up, or worse still be imprisoned!

Over the next few days they spent much of their time in bars, bookies, or drowning what was left of their sorrows back at the house they were sharing. When both were beyond any sensible frame of mind they often fell out, even coming to blows, after which it was not unusual for Hanson to find himself locked out and having to spend the night under the canal bridge to sleep off the effects of his over-indulgence.

On these nights he would come to in the early hours of the morning cold and hungry, and resentful of what he saw as the injustice of Sheppard having both a home and a release from having to fight, when it was clear that this was a man who was keen to do so, whereas he had no real home, no inclination to fight, or any genuine excuse to let him off from service.

If only he had such a document as Sheppard had. The thought crossed his mind to find and steal this, but that wouldn't show his identity and so would be of no use. Anyway, he had no idea where to find it, never a chance of hunting for it, and there was certainly no way Jack would just hand it over to him.

This arrangement went on into the end months of 1916. Just as Syd Hanson was beginning to realise it must be time to move on before he was apprehended by the authorities, something happened to provide him with the opportunity he'd been looking for. The two men had been on a particularly heavy drinking binge that night, following losing substantially betting on card games with others in the pub.

It was as they made their way back along the canal path which took them back to the house, still with bottles in hand, that a row broke out between them as to whose fault it had been that so much money had been lost.

Drinking till the bottles were dry the argument escalated until punches started flying. Neither man would give in though neither could barely stand. The difference between them, with Sheppard originally being of a less aggressive temperament when sober, was mainly in the fact that Hanson, though no taller, was rather more solidly built giving him the advantage. Then of course there was the matter of his quick, uncontrollable temper, and far more aggressive nature.

It was as they passed under the canal bridge that Hanson's temper snapped completely. Grabbing Sheppard firmly by the collar with one hand he then thrust him violently against the wall of the bridge and watched his victim fall to the ground unconscious…or was he dead?

Did he care? It seemed unlikely. After all, he reasoned, he had been provoked. He bent down and took a closer look which told him that Sheppard was still breathing, just. What should he do now? If he reported it or sought help he would most certainly be accused of assault. Neither did he wish to attract unwanted attention to himself. Certainly he would be found out for dodging call up, and at that point in time, after avoiding it this long, that was more important to him than this useless excuse for a man lying at his feet.

Then a thought came to him, a way out of all his troubles perhaps. If Jack was dead and not found he could go back to the house and find the paper absolving him from service. But he was not dead and would be found if left there. Hanson made a snap decision. He felt in the other man's pocket for the door keys and replaced them with a couple of bills with his own name on. With some reluctance he also took out the fob watch he had won in a card game recently and attached it to Sheppard's jacket. He figured that its previous owner would certainly remember that it was Hanson who had won it off of him as they nearly came to blows over it.

Looking around to check there was nobody about he made his decision. After all Syd figured, Jack was unconscious and it would look as if he'd been drinking, tripped, hit his head on the bridge, and fallen into the canal. Nobody would come this way until morning and he could be miles away by then.

There was a loud splash as Jack's body rolled into the water, in no fit state to prevent the inevitable consequence of drowning. In fact, with no other identity save that of Hanson's, it would appear that the body was that of Sydney Hanson. In the eyes of the authorities Mr Sydney Hanson would no longer exist. No one would have reason to associate the body with poor Jack Sheppard.

By the next morning all traces of Jack Sheppard were gone from the house and replaced with those of Sydney Hanson. All there was left was a note to the landlord to say that he, Jack Sheppard, was having to move away for a while, and that his friend, Sydney Hanson, would be left by the end of the week. Just for the sake of appearing the honest man that Jack was, he even went so far as to leave rent to cover till the end of that week.

All he would have to do now was to take on the role and characteristics of Jack Sheppard for the duration of the war, perhaps even beyond for a while, and life would be a doddle, as he looked at it. That shouldn't be so hard after all.

A few weeks later a small article was printed in the local paper to say that 'a body had been retrieved from the canal, presumed drowned whilst intoxicated, and it is believed to be a man by the name of Sydney Hanson of no fixed abode, who neighbours believe to have been staying temporarily with a man named Jack Sheppard', but that Sheppard was believed to have moved away some days before this. According to the police no suspicious circumstances were thought to be involved.

Chapter Nine

Disruption & distress.

John Lawes had been a welcome lodger at the Burgess household now for some months when things were to take an unwelcome change for all there. Toward the end of 1916, William Lawes took a sudden turn for the worse and passed away leaving John as sole owner and manager of the business and all that went with it, including the house in which John had been brought up. This was a particularly grand and spacious house within walking distance of the business.

It appeared to many that it was strange therefore that John had chosen to remain as a lodger in Kate's house on his return, rather than return to live with his father, but the fact was that John had always been extremely close to his mother as he grew up as she was a warm and loving person, but never quite so with his father. Perhaps this may have been to do with William's insistence to pack his son off to boarding school believing this to be the only way to guarantee the type of education he had himself received. Whatever the cause, though John held his father in high esteem, since the death of William's wife Elizabeth the two had found that, apart from the business, they had little in common and found it hard to communicate on a more personal level.

Now the house had become empty John assumed his rightful place as the head of the household. The household in this case consisted of Mrs Betts the housekeeper and cook, a jolly, homely sort of person who had worked there for many years since going there as a young housemaid. Her late husband Alfred had once been employed as butler, but had never been replaced as times had changed and a butler had become an unnecessary extravagance though not so a cook, especially in the household of a widower. She had been running the household as far back as John could remember, back to the days when she took over from an earlier cook. He smiled to himself when he remembered sneaking into the kitchen when he thought Mrs Betts wasn't looking, hoping to snatch an odd homemade biscuit, or stick his finger into a bowl of something tasty, but invariably she would catch him and threaten to 'box his ears', 'tell his mother', or heaven forbid 'tell his father' what he'd been up to. Only this last threat would have any real effect on him though, as he knew that she had something of a soft spot for him and would usually follow up the scolding with some small treat anyway.

There was also Patty, the housemaid, who fulfilled all other assorted roles required of her. Mrs Betts had told Kate that she'd hoped to train Patty up to step into her shoes when the time for retirement came, but now she was beginning to believe this would not work. Young Patty had begun courting a very nice young man. It was early days yet but this could make it difficult for her to stay on as cook. Back in the days when the house had a full complement of servants this was never as difficult as the young man could often be taken on as a footman, under butler, or even perhaps, depending on his appearance and training, a gentleman's valet but those days were long gone, certainly for this household at least. Besides which Patty's young man had been offered a position in a household some way off and they had decided that, once he settled into this, it would be best for them to marry sooner than they had planned to enable them to move away together. At least, Mrs Betts thought, Patty was now skilled enough to perhaps be employed alongside her new husband when the time came, and that at least gave her the satisfaction of knowing that she had taught her the skills she would need to do so.

With Patty gone Mrs Betts was only too pleased to see the return of 'young master John', as she called him. Though she had been happy to serve his father, she could now look forward to keeping a much less formal house perhaps.

With John moving out of the Burgess house, life there became suddenly very quiet, too quiet for Kate and Sarah's liking. Finding themselves alone in the house for the first time in many months, Kate and Sarah continued to find ways to make ends meet. Sarah was now sixteen and had had to find new employment due to the company she had worked for closing down for the duration. She therefore had to look around for any part-time jobs locally to help out temporarily whilst looking for something more permanent. Neither were too proud to take on any work available. Most of this was cleaning or shop work, but they were determined to do whatever it took to pay their way and keep up to date with the rent on the house, and would certainly not dream off demeaning themselves by asking for this to be lowered, even though John Lawes was now their landlord. Of course this fact had never occurred to him either or he most certainly would have been only too pleased to make a suitable reduction for them.

Though no news came both were still praying, as were so many, for this terrible war to end and for dear husband and father, Tom, to be returned to them in one piece. They had had no correspondence from him now since receiving a short, but comforting note he had written following that awful battle of the Somme in which it seemed, so many thousands had died. At least, Kate thought, if he had survived that ordeal, nothing could be worse than that. Surely he would be home safe and sound soon.

But this was not to be. One morning in early October 1917 came a knock on the door, and there stood a young man holding out Kate's worst nightmare.......a telegram!

Without looking at it she knew what it would say. "What is it Mother," called Sarah from the kitchen, but as she came into the hall and saw the tears streaming down her mother's face, she too knew the awful truth of the words on the telegram.

'Sorry to inform you that Sgt Thomas Burgess was killed in action'

All of Kate's strength left her and mother and daughter threw their arms around each other, unable to speak, and cried, oh how they cried! All their hopes and prayers were completely dashed, shattered like glass against concrete. Never to see the man they both loved with such a passion was inconceivable, unbearable. It seemed that life itself had come to an abrupt end; what was the point of it now? How would they ever be able to face life without him?

This was the nightmare faced by so many thousands of wives and families left alone during and after the terrible events, often the unnecessary slaughter on both sides, of the conflict of WW1. Ripped apart by a war brought about by greed and lack of compassion for the ordinary people of many countries by their leaders and politicians.

Left to pick up the pieces and rebuild their shattered lives, women like Kate struggled to cope, but had little choice. By the end of this war the numbers of dead increased from thousands to millions, not just British, but those on both sides of the conflict and of many nationalities. 'The war to end all wars', it was called, but we know now this was not to be.

Towards the end of 1917 Kate receive a brief but poignant letter from an officer of Tom's regiment who had served with him. In this he explained to Kate that, due to such heavy losses at the second battle of Ypres, much of this due to the first use of poisonous gas amongst the trenches, Tom had been quickly promoted to sergeant due to his ability to organise and inspire the younger men serving under him. He had apparently been a true inspiration and a calming influence to them when they most needed it.

Even so, having fought through the disastrous battle of the Somme the previous year, even Tom's influence was unable to hold them together when the fighting reached such ferocity that it is said that there were around 700,000 killed and wounded.

It had been this which had been the cause of Tom's death. Typical of his character, as he tried to calm his men in their trench, the youngest lad of the group, just seventeen years old, had panicked and leapt out to make a run for it. Without hesitation Sgt Tom Burgess had also leapt out and thrown himself on the lad in an attempt to shield him from enemy fire, but had unfortunately been hit himself. Both men had been hit, the younger one died screaming for his mother.

Tom's men had managed to reach far enough out to drag him back into the trench, but it was clear it was too late to save him.

In his last minutes Tom especially begged his officer to promise to tell 'his girls', 'I love them both', and to add that he was, 'sorry I never mended that door'.

Chapter Ten

New Jobs

Now Kate was a widow and, without the prospect of a return to some form of the old normality, had to decide once again how to make ends meet on a more permanent footing. After some time trying her best to come to terms with what had happened and faced with the reality of her situation she decided to try once again to find another lodger. After all, they had such a positive experience with both Annie and Mr Lawes, and they really had to find a solution to the money worries they were beginning to see looming up at them.

Being a practical and determined young lady, Sarah stopped what she saw as messing around with the low paid part-time jobs she'd been doing and, much to her Mothers disapproval, applied and acquired a job in one of the dreaded munitions factories, that belonging to William Lawes & Son. At least, she explained to Kate, the wage would be guaranteed, more than she'd been earning and, more importantly, regular.

This did mean leaving the house just after five each morning, and often not returning until late after what could be up to a twelve hour shift.

Sarah was not alone in taking such work. Due to the drastic shortage around the country in manpower, women were employed by the hundreds to step into the breach, providing the urgently needed ammunition for the forces.

Worried about her daughter taking on such work Kate sat one evening questioning Sarah,

"Are you sure you can cope with this work dear? I have heard it is so hard. I'm sure we could cope if you find it too much."

Kate's one wish had been to prevent her daughter from turning to factory work if this was at all possible. She had seen the effect this had on those taking on such work.

"No Mother, stop worrying. I'm tougher than you give me credit for, and I get to work alongside plenty of other girls my age. I'll be fine."

At first this was the case, but it soon began to take its toll on her. Not only were the hours long but the work was heavy, repetitive and extremely noisy. Plus there was also considerable danger involved in this work. These workers were handling TNT and other harmful chemicals, running the risk of lethal side effects, and without any of the health and safety precautions which would be insisted on now.

Kate had heard terrible tales of accidents incurred by those girls taking on such work from the dangerous machinery they had to work with. It had been known for hair, or even hands, to get caught in this, causing awful injuries. The chemicals which were used in the making of the munitions also was extremely hazardous to their health. These would eventually cause toxic jaundice which, apart from the obvious risk to health, would turn their skin and hair yellow. For this reason these girls earnt the name of 'canary girls'.

Kate enquired whether Sarah had seen Mr Lawes since starting work at his factory, but Sarah explained that she had been interviewed and taken on by the foreman and that, though she did see him pass by at a distance on one occasion, he tended to spend most of his time upstairs in his office.

Secretly, though she said nothing to Kate, she missed his company around the house.

Chapter Eleven.

The New Lodger.

Kate herself felt she had not the heart or strength to follow her daughter into the factory, but instead took over a couple of Sarah's part-time jobs. These both consisted of cleaning two local shops after closing time. Neither paid so well, meaning that, between them and Sarah's wage, thing were still rather tight on her budget.

Consequently back went the card into the shop window and within a fortnight she had an application from a man by the name of Jack Sheppard. Sheppard was much older than John Lawes, similar age to Tom Burgess. As with John, he seemed keen to explain to her why he had not gone off to join the services, but in his case he claimed to have been unfit for service due to respiratory difficulties from time spent working in mines in his younger days, a story which was later to prove as unreliable as its teller. Strangely, Kate could see no real sign of any such condition but, trusting as she was, was prepared to believe him. He now claimed to have been working as a sales representative, travelling throughout the midlands, but had now found a more settled job in a brewery in the district and was therefore in need of a quiet place to stay until he could acquire something more permanent.

As soon as Syd Hanson, or as he was now know, Jack Sheppard, met Kate Burgess he could see that, from his point of view, he was onto a good thing here. After all, he thought, moving in with a middle class widow and daughter with a very comfortable house had to be good. Up until now the only women he'd had dealings with were what he called scrubbers, or prostitutes, but now he saw possibilities he'd not dreamt of before. All he had to do was play his cards right, bide his time, and he'd reap the benefits.

From the time Jack Sheppard moved in things seemed fine. In fact Jack couldn't have been kinder and more caring towards Kate and her daughter. Still, Kate found life without Tom unbearable. She knew nobody could ever take his place in her heart, and the thought of spending the rest of her life without him seemed frightening. Sheppard soon became aware of this and worked hard on ingratiating himself to her, aiming to become invaluable to what he saw as a very lonely, possibly even a little desperate widow, living in such a place he could never aspire to on his own, and certainly somewhere he could make himself comfortable with very little effort. Maybe, he decided, this was the fresh start he needed, the one he thought he always wanted. After all, life until now had dealt him a pretty poor hand. This time he would be a reformed character and enjoy the life he felt he deserved!

He would go off each morning with the snap Kate prepared for him under his arm and return home regularly at six o'clock every evening. He would sit and happily enjoy the evening meal shared by the three of them, although there were often days when Kate had to keep Sarah's meal warm as she was working late.

On these days he always seemed more than pleased to chat to Kate as they ate, after which he would busy himself in the back yard chopping kindling for the fire and filling the coal scuttle to keep the fire going for the evening as she saw to washing the pots and plates from the meal.

Life continued in this vein, even gradually stretching to the odd stroll in the park on the odd weekend. By the time Jack had been in the Burgess house for nearly six weeks Kate had come to the conclusion that, though he was nothing like John Lawes, and certainly nothing like her beloved Tom, he seemed perfectly trustworthy, even quite pleasant.

Sarah though was not convinced. When she said as much to Annie on one of her occasional visits, Annie, not having actually met Jack yet, said that,

"Perhaps the reason you feel that way is that you're comparing him with you Pa. After all there's not many men can compare to him you know."

"I suppose you're probably right Annie. Still, I don't feel altogether comfortable with the way he's worked his way into Mother's affection, doesn't seem right."

Perhaps, she thought on her way home, just perhaps I'm just acting like a petulant kid. After all, Mother can choose for herself who she likes, it's not up to me as long as she's happy.

Even so, Sarah felt uncomfortable somehow, especially with Jack making what she felt was unnecessary effort to endear himself to her mother, particularly at this time when Kate was in such a vulnerable state after her loss.

However, before long her mind was taken off of these thoughts by the predicament which was soon to face Annie. Three weeks into the new lodger moving into the Burgess household, Mrs Hackett fell ill and was taken into the infirmary. This left poor Annie, whose father had returned from the war in a somewhat weakened state, not only helping with the children in between work, but having to take full responsibility for them much of the time. Though Sam was working by now of course, and Susie was nearly of an age to leave school, at present she and the three younger children were still at home and had to be fed, clothed and packed off to school every day, and still allow time for Annie to earn a living and occasionally visit their mother in the infirmary. Luckily her employer was happy for her to take home enough work to do to help pay the worst of the bills, though all but the barest necessities had to be forgone.

Sarah decided that under the circumstances the least she could do was to move in with Annie to give what support she could when not at work, and give just a little toward the family budget.

"No Sarah, you don't need to do that. I'm sure we can cope," Annie was quick to assure her, "Besides, you have your own job to go to, and your ma would hate not having you at home."

"I've made up my mind, so it's no use you arguing," Sarah told her, "Anyway it was Mother who suggested it in the first place."

She was quite right. When they had discussed poor Mrs Hackett's illness, and the predicament this had left Annie in, Kate was quick to insist that,

"After all Sarah, my income is much improved since Jack moved in, and with five children, a job and a house to maintain, poor Annie really needs some help from someone."

And so it was agreed.

Chapter Twelve.

Changes.

This new arrangement suited Jack well. Being left alone in the house with Kate meant that he could work on his relationship with her without having to ingratiate himself to Sarah at the same time. By being on his best behaviour, added to Kate's vulnerability, and being on hand to help with all the duties normally expected of the man of the house, he soon made himself appear indispensable to her.

Though it took all his persuasion she even accepted his offer to go with him to the Royal Oak public house two streets away on the occasional Friday night, after he received his pay.

"Please think about it Kate, you need to get your life back again," he implored her after Sarah had been gone for a couple of weeks, "I understand you've been mourning your poor dear husband, but I'm sure he wouldn't want to see you fading away, and wasting your life like this for so long."

And so Kate was persuaded to don her second best coat and hat (the very best being just for church on Sundays), take Jack's arm, and be escorted to the Royal Oak where he would treat her to a weekly glass of sherry. She had never taken to drinking half-pints of ale or shandy as some other women did, but found that, after so long, it was a relief to get out and meet other women for a chat whilst the men talked amongst themselves, or played darts in the corner.

Jack appeared to Kate to drink in reasonable moderation on these occasions, in fact she thought, she had not seen him drunk since he arrived at her home. She was relieved at this especially as Tom had never been a big drinker. She didn't think she could cope with a man in the house who came in roaring drunk as she knew many did, but Jack gave the appearance of a sober and reliable individual, one she quickly begun to feel at home with.

Often at weekends he would go walking in the park with her and on the weekends when Sarah popped back to see her mother, Kate would pack a picnic to share. She could sense a certain unease on her daughter's part, but thought this was only natural as Sarah had been so very close to her father. Hopefully this tension would lessen in time, Kate was convinced of that.

For his part Jack found himself having to struggle with his temper when Sarah was about. This wasn't what he'd planned for. He rather had hoped that she would by now have moved in permanently with the Hackett's, or even found a man of her own to keep her out of his way. Getting round Kate he had found difficult, but given the depth of her loneliness since becoming widowed, put her in a far more vulnerable position, and therefore worth working on. The daughter on the other hand was impervious to his attempts to charm her, a fact which could completely scupper his peaceful, easy going life. In fact, right from the start, he had never really liked the girl at all, though he had to admit to himself that with her fair hair and blue eyes she was 'a bit of a looker' and no mistake. Still, he decided, you can't have both, at least not with her attitude.

When Kate suggested one week that she should invite Sarah along with them to the Royal Oak Jack was fuming. Taking her totally by surprise, he turned on her with a look of pure rage on his face,

"No you bloody well shouldn't," and then, realising the effect his outburst had had on Kate, forced the best semblance of a smile to his face before giving an equally forced laugh to his next words, "Don't look so shocked dear, you know I was just joking. Of course she's welcome to come."

Later that evening while she waited for Sarah to come in as she did every Friday after work, Jack's outburst, joke or otherwise, went round in her mind, leaving her feeling still rather shaken. Tom had never once raised his voice to her, in fact she didn't think he'd ever have raised his voice like that to anyone. Still, Jack had said he'd just been joking, and had assured her that Sarah would be welcome to join them one weekend.

Consequently, while mother and daughter sat sharing a good warming and satisfying helping of Kate's cottage pie, a favourite of Sarah's, her mother brought up the subject of the proposed outing. This was the first Sarah had heard of her mother's trips to the pub, and she couldn't help thinking this to be very unlike her. She couldn't imagine her father taking her to such a place.

Kate read her daughters expression and quickly assured her that the Royal Oak was a perfectly respectable place, not like ones the men frequented alone. There were, she assured Sarah, quite a little gathering of wives there most Friday nights.

Sarah had to give in in the end and agree that, after all she had been through, her mother did deserve a chance of a little renewed happiness in her life. Still, she had something of a job convincing herself that Jack was the man to provide this. Perhaps she should go along just to put her mind at rest.

Therefore, the following Friday after work, Sarah rushed back to Annie's to clean up and put on a tidy set of clothes. "Are you sure you're ok with me going out tonight? I feel mean leaving you here while I go gallivanting, but I do feel worried about Mother, and about his influence on her."

Annie threw her friend a look of exasperation and said with a laugh in her voice, "You're supposed to be the daughter, not the mother! Will you stop worrying, I'm sure your mother knows what she's doing; and I'm sure he's not as bad as you make him out to be."

By the end of the evening Sarah had to admit that things had gone well and that, as Annie had suggested, her worries had been quite unfounded. Yet, in spite of seeing Jack Sheppard on his best behaviour and her mother more relaxed than she'd seen her for some time, she somehow knew she would never completely trust him.

After this evening Sarah would accompany Kate and Jack occasionally on their Saturday evenings out. Apart from enjoying her mother's company, she felt it also allowed her to keep an eye on Jack. She would go back and report each event to Annie, though still keeping to herself the constant underlying feeling of unease which, try as she might, just kept hovering in the back of her mind.

After all, she thought, it seemed it was just her who was suspicious of the new lodger. Even so, she decided that on the weekends when both Annie and Sam were home to take care of the youngsters, there was really no need not to use that as an excuse to pop home for an odd day or two.

Chapter Thirteen.

Making his move.

Jack Sheppard had by now lived in Kate's house as a lodger for almost a year. Though he'd found it something of a struggle at times to try to convert into an entirely different character, he did genuinely work hard to do so, realising that this was the only hope he would ever get to hang on to this new easy existence he'd not experienced before.

What he found as hard as trying to gain Sarah's trust was also trying to gain the trust and respect of the neighbours, Bill and May. Not that he really cared what they thought of him, but it seemed to be important to Kate, and so he did try…at least at first.

On one of their early visits to the Royal Oak with Kate, Bill and May had also been there. Kate had been quick to call them over and introduce them to Jack.

"Good to meet you Jack," said Bill, shaking him firmly by the hand, "Are you going to be staying around here for long mate?"

"For the foreseeable future, as far as I know anyway," Jack told him with as much casual indifference as he could muster.

When he went off to the bar to order drinks for himself and Kate he found Bill had come up to join him, insisting on buying drinks for the four of them,

"Give us chance to get to know you Jack, we're very fond of Kate and young Sarah, and it's good to know they've got a man in the house to help them out and look after them. It were a real tragedy, what happened to poor Tom. Such a smashing chap he were too."

By the end of the evening Jack's temper had been pushed to its limit. He'd planned on a quiet night at the pub with Kate, possibly an odd game of darts with a couple of lads there who just played without pestering him, but instead he'd had to put up with what to him was the inane gossip, and even more, the unwanted questioning, of this ridiculous couple from next door!

In fact, the only saving grace of the evening was that this was not a night when Sarah came too. Even so, having walked home in silence, and at such a pace that Kate found it hard to keep up, he refused the cup of cocoa which Kate always made them before turning in, and took himself of upstairs with just the barest 'goodnight'.

What he was unaware of was of course that the other side of the adjoining wall, Bill was saying to May,

"I don't reckon much to that Jack. Seems a bit shifty to me."

When May asked why, all he could say was that, "I don't rightly know, just don't reckon I'd trust him as far as I could throw him. Suppose there's not much we can do about it, its Kate's house, she must know what she's doing."

In spite of finding it difficult trying to make a good impression on her friends, Jack was determined to do the best he could and not allow them to come between him and his ultimate plan.

Therefore, after what he considered to be a suitable length of time Sheppard coaxed and cajoled Kate into marrying him. After all she decided, possibly with a little discreet prompting from Jack himself, she had now been on her own for nearly two years and realised that at the age of forty this might be the last chance to find security for herself and her daughter. Though she could never love him as she had Tom, at this point at least, Jack certainly seemed respectable enough, and had given her no reason to doubt his sincerity. She convinced herself, as she was to realise much later to her cost, that this was the right thing to do. Her friends could see she was doing it out of desperation and tried to warn her about him, but he had been persistent and quite expert at hiding his true character.

Therefore, somewhat reluctantly, Sarah duly attended the brief ceremony at the registry office in Birmingham, along with Annie and May, both of whom acted as witnesses. It was a fairly brief and discreet affair, Kate almost feeling disloyal to Tom's memory by remarrying, but Jack at least felt a sense of relief and achievement in making it legal and binding. Not only had he now gained a wife to attend to all his needs, but being the man of the house also made him the primary householder. His life was complete, and with so little effort!

As if to prove the doubters wrong he had made a special effort at the beginning to look the perfect husband, in public at least showing only his good qualities. Every weekday morning he would eat the breakfast Kate prepared for him, packed the sandwiches she wrapped into the bag he always took with him, apparently to keep his paperwork in, and with a quick peck on her cheek would set off to work. Every evening he would return, often looking a little worse for wear due, he told Kate, to his condition and to the pressure of work and amount of travel he had to fit into each day.

"Don't worry yourself about me my dear," he told her on one occasion, "it's just been a long day. You won't mind if I use that desk I've seen in the cellar to catch up on a few things before we eat would you?"

Just briefly Kate looked quite taken aback… that was Tom's desk, in Tom's office. No one except her had been down there hardly since he died and, with the exception of John Lawes on just a few occasions, certainly not used his desk. Though she wasn't comfortable with the idea and could not see what use he would have for a desk, she reasoned that she was being silly feeling this way. After all, Jack was her husband now, and there was no real reason why he shouldn't be allowed to have a little private space to unwind after a day's work.

And so it was agreed. "Just remember when you go down to either leave the door open, or hook the string up to stop the latch dropping, or you might get stuck if I'm not around to open it from outside!" she said in as light hearted a voice as she could muster, remembering Tom's last message to her.

Chapter Fourteen.

True Colours.

Now with the passage of time circumstances had changed. It became obvious to all who met him that this was a man who preferred to live off the earnings and achievements of his predecessor than trouble himself to seek any of his own.

Once Jack Sheppard had his feet firmly under their table he had begun to show a completely different side of his character to his new family. It seemed he no longer had to go off of a morning to work every day. True he did sometimes go off after breakfast, though Kate was not sure exactly where he went on those occasions. His working hours seemed very erratic with him coming and going at different times of the day, sometimes even at night. In fact he was out often for a greater part of the evening as well, a fact that really puzzled Kate and Sarah as he had never before seemed to have worked so late in the day.

It could be said that they were rather naïve when it came to men of this kind. Compared to Tom this was an unwelcome change. "I really can't understand why Jack is suddenly so short tempered,"

Kate told her friend Mrs Betts, "he seems so unpredictable lately, not at all like he was when we married."

Sarah resisted the temptation to tell Annie 'I told you so.' Although she would have been within her rights to do so, she was still not certain they had seen the worst of him yet. Just what the worst could possibly be she genuinely had not the slightest idea. All she did know was that she felt the need to move back in to be with her mother.

Mrs Hackett was now home at last and, though still rather weak, could just about cope with help from Annie and Sam, and so Sarah resumed her place in her childhood home, hoping to support mother in her new life, a move which did not go down well with her new 'step-father'.

Naturally, Kate worried that Jack's change in character was being brought about by something she was doing, but tried hard not to make Sarah aware of her worries. Had she spoken to her daughter about this she would have found that Sarah didn't need telling as she had seen the changes for herself. In their own minds they both decided, or perhaps just hoped that maybe it was just the pressure of his work, or sometimes even the lack of, that was the cause of his strange behaviour. Obviously, Sarah thought, his work wasn't bringing in an amount to sustain him as she was aware of him not contributing what they had expected toward the rent, and taking (very often without asking), much of the pittance her mother brought in from the few pounds a week she received from her employment at the local grocery shop in the next street to make up the difference.

Of course Sarah also paid her share into the family coffers, yet still there always seemed a shortfall each time the rent fell due.

This became a real concern to Kate in particular as the idea of having to move out of what had been their family home for some time now seemed unthinkable. After all, her best memories of dear Tom were centred on this house.

Of late they both had noticed that he would come in, barely grunting an acknowledgement to either his wife or step-daughter, and disappear straight into the cellar. Sarah did wonder whether he was following in father's footsteps and using this as a space to do some sort of paperwork, though they couldn't imagine what that would be, but neither dared ask to what use he was putting poor Tom's 'office'. At least, Kate told her daughter, better for him to be allowed a space to himself, away from a house with two women in it, a space to unwind, and anyway, if it left him in a better frame of mind by the time he emerged, that was all to the good.

Although Kate had taken the precaution of telling him, when he was in a more approachable frame of mind shortly after their marriage, about the risks involved in allowing the door to shut without ensuring the loop of string was suitably attached to the bolt, this was still something which just added to his explosive bouts of rage. Early on in their marriage, while he was still trying to make an impression on her, he also had said he would fix it but, needless to say, had never done so, yet many were the times when either Kate or Sarah would be alerted to his plight by Jack's loud shouting and hammering on the door when the inevitable lock-in occurred.

Of course this could have been avoided had he bothered to do the repair needed, yet in fact all he had done since making that promise was to tell both Kate and Sarah in no uncertain terms that they were not to enter the cellar as this was his space now and that, when he was in there he wanted to be left alone.

Sarah couldn't help feeling saddened by this, but both she and her mother sensed that it would not be wise to question or to cross him over it. Luckily she had by this time found herself employment a bus ride away that meant she didn't spend too much time at home except for evenings and weekends. Though this was factory work of a kind she found unbearably boring, yet less unpleasant than the war work she had been doing in the Lawes factory, at least she managed to avoid her stepfather and his increasingly short tempered ways. Never the less she hated leaving mother alone and, as she saw it, at his mercy, especially when he came home in one of his black moods.

"I know you think it's just me being silly again," she told Annie, "but I can't seem to bring myself to trust him, whatever you say." This time Annie made little attempt to convince her friend as she had been there on one occasion when Jack had come home in what she could see was a foul mood.

During this time Sarah had begun to allow Sam the privilege of walking her home from time to time. Though he was just a little younger in years, the necessity of having to grow up so fast due to their family circumstance had made him so much more mature than many lads his age. Having also spent much time around one another whilst Mrs Hackett was ill, it seemed quite natural to Sarah to be at ease with him now.

To start with Sam would meet her on her way home from work and, making an effort to have this look almost accidental, took the long route home so that he could escort her to hers first. At first Sarah was a little worried that the neighbours might be watching, but then she thought, if it was all they had to amuse themselves then they must live pretty dull lives, so why spoil their pleasure!

"Well, suppose I better be off sharpish like," Sam said each time they got to Sarah's house, "Me Ma will have me tea on the table getting cold if I don't get going. Night girl, perhaps see you tomorrow."

Since the war, with Mr Hackett gradually getting weaker from the effects of the gas used in the trenches by the enemy, Sam had had to grow up fast, almost having to act as man of the house by now.

Gradually they found they were spending more time together, though usually in the company of Annie, taking the younger Hackett's out for a while sometimes to allow Mrs Hackett more time to care for her husband's needs, without having the youngsters constantly bickering and generally making a noise.

"Bet folk think we're a funny looking family," remarked Annie one day in the park, "Must look like a chap with two wives and four kids," and both Sam and Sarah, given a second or two to consider her viewpoint, both roared with laughter.

Though Sam found himself particularly fond of Sarah, in the back of her mind he would never be quite the man of her girlish dreams but, until she perhaps was lucky enough to meet someone based on this 'fantasy man', at least Sam was kind and seemed genuinely pleased to be around her.

Seeing this friendship appearing to blossom Kate was more than happy to encourage it. To Sarah, almost too keen to do so. "Why don't you ask Sam in for tea one day dear? It's good to see you with someone your own age."

For two reasons her mother's suggestion was not one that Sarah immediately leapt at. Firstly, she felt it might be rather unfair to give poor Sam the wrong idea about just what her feelings for him were. She wasn't sure herself really as she'd had little experience of other lads, so were these the feelings she must accept? And then there was the worrying thought of bringing him into the house to meet Jack. She felt somehow rather concerned that this could go badly. After all, Jack was so moody of late, and seemed unhappy about having visitors to what he now spoke of as 'my house'. Even so, with a bit of coaxing from Kate, Sam was duly invited to come back to eat with them one evening.

Things went well that first time. Kate had prepared a good warming beef stew, knowing that that was usually something that men all seemed to enjoy. Jack had come home at a reasonable time and sat at the table keen to show himself off as the head of the family. Sarah managed to relax and feel perhaps her worries had been unfounded, and even Jack was on his best behaviour that night. Little did she realise that he saw this budding relationship of hers as a way to get her out of the house for good.

He quizzed Sam about his work, and in return went to lengths to rave to their visitor about the amazing job he'd managed to find at the brewery since coming here. In fact the only time Kate noticed with trepidation the slightest twinge of the temper she knew by now he had was when Sam brought up the subject of the war.

"See, that's why me Pa can't work now, cos of the gas you know. Got to his lungs they say. What did you do in the war Mr Sheppard?"

For what seemed to Kate like a terrible, almost terrifying few seconds, Jack stopped eating and glared at the lad. Scared of what he might do next she decided to try diversionary tactics in the hope of distracting her husband from whatever he might do,
"More stew Jack, and how about you young Sam. I'm sure the two of you can clear up the last of it between you now?"

Realising he was at risk of blowing his plan to get Sarah out of the house, Jack let himself be side-tracked for once, "Sure we can do that for you my love, we men need feeding up if we're going to provide for our ladies, eh Sam?"

In answer to Sam's question all he said was that he'd already got lung problems before the war so was not fit to fight. Sam for his part was not convinced.

Chapter Fifteen.

Worsening Times.

It was not very long before Sam became aware of this feeling his sister relayed to him about Sarah's new step father, and promised Annie, "I'll keep an eye on him when I'm with Sarah."

With that in mind he made a point of increasing the times when he would walk her home. Though Sarah had made her mind up not to encourage him too much, she had to admit to herself if nobody else that in a way she couldn't quite put her finger on, Sam's company as she entered the house did seem a comfort to her.

On the other hand, from Mr Hackett's view point, this relationship the pair appeared to be forming didn't altogether sit well in his mind.

"You know lad," he put to his son one evening, "I don't hold with you spending so much time hanging around with that lass."

"What's wrong with it, why you so against it? Sarah's been good to us all while me ma has been poorly, and I reckon we're good together," Sam could feel the hackles on his neck rise when he realised just how strongly his father felt against his growing attachment to Sarah. "Anyway, I reckon I'm old enough to choose for myself who I spend my time with."

Mr Hackett could see a determination he'd not seen before from his son, almost a look of sheer defiance. Fixing Sam with an equally determined look, Mr Hackett rose from his chair and, taking a step in Sam's direction, shook a finger in the boy's face saying, "Now you listen here lad, and listen good. All the time you're living under my roof you'll mind what I say, and I say you're not to set your cap at that girl."

"She's not 'that girl', she's Sarah, and why the hell shouldn't I? She's plenty good enough for me if she'd have me one day, and..."

"That's just my point, she's too bloody good. Too good for the likes of our sort with her Pa having been an educated man as he was. How long do you reckon she'd be happy with the life you could give her? No; not while you're under my roof do you talk any more of such rubbish."

Sam had never before defied his father, but this time he'd made up his mind to follow his own conscience and ambition. "Right Pa, if that's really how you feel, perhaps it's nearly time I moved out, find a place away from here to be."

"And you reckon she'd come with you lad, and where you gonna get the money to do that then?" This remark of Mr Hackett's was more than his son could take right at this time. Sam walked from the room and out of the back door, slamming it hard behind him!

As the weeks went on nothing more was said on the subject. Mrs Hackett and the rest of the family never heard about this exchange between father and son. Sam carried on 'accidently' meeting Sarah, who, in her turn, would be glad of his company to walk her home, and had begun to invite him in from time to time for a cup of tea to refresh him for his remaining walk home. Or at least that was what she told him, and what he chose to believe.

The truth of the matter from Sarah's point of view was actually a little more involved than just a refreshment stop, or certainly the gradual blossoming of the friendship Sam had hoped to nurture.

The real truth behind her invitation was really a matter of support, though just for what purpose she wasn't certain. It was just a feeling of unease she sometimes felt entering the house alone, almost as if she was scared of what she might find on the other side of the door. Probably her concerns were totally unfounded, but she was aware of a change of the relaxed ease she had always felt speaking to her mother. Since father had gone they had become closer than ever, held together initially by the grief they shared. But now Sarah felt her mother seemed somewhat reserved and guarded in the way she spoke, and the subject matter she seemed to want to share with her daughter. This reserve not only hurt Sarah's feelings, but caused her great concern.

This became even more concerning one day when Sarah came home a little early to find Kate quickly pulling on a cardigan to cover a nasty bruise on her arm.

"How ever did you do that," she asked, but was told by Kate that she had just been a little clumsy and caught it on the kitchen door handle. Even so, it did seem that mother was becoming increasingly clumsy if Sarah was to believe that excuse as after that first time she couldn't help noticing the odd bruise or two appearing without any logical explanation…at least none that made any sense!

Chapter Sixteen.

Rising Temper.

For some time now Sheppard had tried hard to control both his temper and his bad ways knowing that he couldn't risk any encounter with the police for fear of having his comfortable new lifestyle brought to an abrupt halt. But being a man of weak character he eventually found himself creeping back to his old habits. After all, the war was over now so there was less chance of being in trouble over his avoidance of military service, and anyway, he still had the paperwork to say he was exempt from this. On that basis he was less concerned to keep up the front he'd built up and began to let his guard down now and again, reverting more and more to the ways of a certain Sydney Hanson!

He would come home a little the worse for wear, carrying his work bag under his arm, obviously so much heavier than when he had left home, and go straight into the cellar. Kate would have a meal prepared for him, but could never be sure what response she would get when she called him to eat it. If he did come to the table he would shovel the food down, make disgusting noises and leave, never caring if Kate and Sarah had started, let alone finished! Some days he just wouldn't bother coming to eat at all. There was even a couple of occasions when the meal in front of him was not to his liking and he shouted abuse and hurled it across the room, leaving mother and daughter to clean up the mess!

On one occasion Kate made what was perhaps a silly mistake, of trying to make light conversation by asking him for his opinion on the new recipe she had tried. Without warning Sheppard picked up his half empty plate, shouted some expletives at his wife, and once again launched the plate across the room, this time aiming it at Kate but narrowly missing Sarah's head in the process! Without a word of apology he got up from the table and marched off down the hall to the cellar, slamming the door behind him.

Usually again it was down to Kate to follow him along to the cellar door and see that the latch was safely hooked up. Once or twice she forgot to do so and he found himself locked in. She was alerted to his plight by him hammering on the door and shouting such obscene language that Kate rushed to his aid fearing the neighbours might hear. This happened one Saturday when Sarah was home and, though she was on her way to release him, mother was ahead of her and insisted that Sarah should stay out of his way when he was like this.

She watched as Kate opened the door and her step-father came out like a raging bull,
"You useless bitch, you lock that damn door on me again and I'll smash your bloody head in," as he said this grabbing her by her arm and hurling her across the hall.
Now Sarah could see where her mother's 'clumsiness' was coming from!

Both mother and daughter were shaken to the core, both scared of how much worse things could possibly get, but little did they know the true extent of what was to come.

At this stage Sarah decided to ask Kate if she might ask Sam to stay for a meal a couple of times a week, her excuse, should she have needed it, that it would help poor Mrs Hackett with the expense of feeding as many mouths so often. The truth behind her invitation really was the hope that having another man, even one so young, join them, this may help Jack feel less outnumbered by the females in the house and therefore act a little less aggressively towards them.

"Of course you can dear, but just warn him that your step-father can be a little short tempered, so be careful not to provoke him in any way."

Naturally, Sam jumped at the chance to stay over, not so much for the meal (though being a lad with a good appetite this was much appreciated), but mostly because he hoped the invitation meant Sarah must like his company as much as he liked hers. It was agreed that he should stay twice a week, Mondays and Fridays, an arrangement which evoked very different feelings in different people.

Mr Hackett was fuming when his wife told him what was suggested. "What the hell's he think he's doing? Damn stupid little bugger, I told him to stop this nonsense before it got too far. No good'll come of it and he knows it."

"Don't be so hard on him Pa," Annie tried to speak up for her brother. "I don't reckon he's doing it for the reason you think. I reckon from what Sarah's been telling me, that step-father of hers has been getting a bit nasty lately, and she thinks having another man there sometimes might help."

"That's just my point…he's not a man, not yet. He's still a boy, and a pretty daft one at that if he reckons he can get round her, let alone deal with her old man." Mr Hackett threw his cigarette end in the fire and stormed out of the room.

"What do you think Ma," asked Annie.

"As far as your Pa's view on his fancy for Sarah, I have to agree it doesn't feel right somehow, as much as I love the girl like one of you, but perhaps that's why it don't feel right. It'd be a bit like him walking out with his sister, let alone any idea of it going further. But on the other hand, if it's just to give Sarah and her Ma a bit of support, then I'm all for it."

Kate wasn't altogether sure which way to view the idea of Sam's visits. She was quite fond of all of the Hackett children, and Sam had grown up into a very nice young boy. Though it never occurred to her that he had any other ambition than to be a good friend to her daughter, she was happy to invite him to join them on these two days a week. One more mouth made little difference after all, especially on the days Jack chose not to bother eating with them. She did though also think there was just a chance Sarah might be right about the effect another male presence might have on her husband's moods, hopefully for the better.

And so it was decided, to everybody's mix of emotions that Sam would eat with them Mondays and Fridays after work.

For a while to both mother and daughter, it did seem that having Sam there on those days did have some bearing on Jack's behaviour. In fact, not being aware of his ulterior motive, they were quite surprised at the effort he appeared to put into befriending the lad.

Chapter Seventeen

Discoveries.

For all his apparent efforts at friendship with Sam, this did not extend to his wife and step-daughter. It soon became clear to Kate what a terrible situation she had, through her grief at losing Tom, put both herself and her daughter in. Clearly she would have been far better to remain a widow than to bring such a man into the house. Naïve she may have been at first, but totally ignorant of men she was not. It soon became apparent that her new husband was nothing but a lazy, dishonest drunkard. She also could see that much of the money she and Sarah brought into the house went back out to pay for drink and gambling.

She now felt sure that, even from early on, he was otherwise in perfectly good health and as such could see no legitimate reason why he should not have been serving in the forces. If dear Tom could go and serve his country, even die for it, why not Jack Sheppard? She had made her mind up that he was just a coward through and through, for after all he certainly wasn't the man he made himself out to be at the start.

If only she had realised this when he first arrived, and knew how her life with him would be. She would most certainly have reported him to the authorities, but now that the war was over she doubted they would be interested. And anyway she must be wrong about that she supposed as, when a man in a uniform came to the door not long after their wedding, Jack had produced the paper to show him, proving that 'Jack Sheppard' had applied for service but been turned down as unfit. He had made a point of showing it to her at the same time. Had it been this rejection that had turned him into such a monster? Either way Kate now felt trapped and more miserable than she had ever felt in her life. All she could do now was to protect her daughter from him to the best of her ability.

To make matters worse, one evening when he had rejected the dinner Kate dished up for him and instead gone straight back out within an hour of coming in, Sarah asked her mother, "What do you think he does in Pa's office?", as she still referred to the cellar.

"I really don't know dear, but I think we can be pretty certain he doesn't do any accounts. Last time I suggested going down to give it a sweep he went mad."

Sarah, being more rebellious than her mother, couldn't resist the challenge. "We should go down and look. After all it's our house too, and that was Father's office. Come on, while he's out."

With great trepidation, but feeling just a little emboldened in the knowledge that Jack had only just gone out, probably for the rest of the evening, Kate followed Sarah along the hall. Having first safely secured the string to keep the door from trapping them, they descended the steps down into the 'office'. Before Sarah could reach to turn on the light, she found herself tripping over something glass on the floor.

Kate managed to get to the light first while her daughter recovered her footing. Both women looked around them in horror! All around there were empty bottles stacked in corners, or rolling about across the floor.

Even worse soon became apparent. "Oh no…how could he?"

Kate turned around to see what had upset her daughter so. All Tom's books and papers had been torn up and were scattered across the floor, showing a total disregard for the man they both loved and missed so very much.

Sarah stood amongst them with tears pouring down her face. "How could he," she repeated, "I hate that man. I wish it was him who was dead, not my father."

"I know dear, I know just how you feel dear. I wish we'd not come down here now. Come on, let's go back up before he comes. We must try to remember Father for what he was, not just for what he did here. Nothing can take our memories of him away, certainly not Jack Sheppard. He's not half the man your father was dear." Kate resisted the temptation to make any attempt to do anything about the mess around them. All she wanted now was to get back up the stairs quickly in case her husband returned and caught them there.

Chapter Eighteen.

Kate's Shame.

As far as Sheppard was concerned life was just how he liked it. Knowing he had a home for life, already paid for at that, he knew he had fallen squarely on his feet. He would go out drinking and gambling with those he called his "friends" until they too tired of his excesses. When this happened he drank alone from an ample supply he had accumulated in the cellar and, if he didn't drink enough to render himself unconscious, invariably felt the need to force his unwelcome attentions on poor Kate. Any resistance on her part would drive him to such violence that she dared not show her face outside until the tell-tale bruising faded. He would even go to the extent of ripping her clothing from her back if she was too slow to remove them when he demanded she should do so.

She had never experienced anything like this sort of violence before. When she first married Tom she had been very young and very innocent in such matters, but Tom being the kind and gentle man that he was, had coaxed her along gently allowing her to take as much time as she needed to feel ready for such things.

This was totally different. The force and total lack of respect for either her feelings or her dignity, and most times the pain she suffered on these occasions was beyond anything she had ever believed possible.

Again she tried hard to hide this from Sarah who, though she could tell how unhappy and how often her mother appeared to be covered in bruises, was protected from the real extent of Kate's more personal pain which was always well hidden from her. Kate could not talk about such things to her sweet daughter. After all, Sarah had never even had more than a brief and very innocent relationship with a young man at work, but this had gone no further than a sneaky kiss under the mistletoe at the Christmas party before he left to move away from the area.

After all, just how could she speak of this matter to anyone, let alone her daughter? On one occasion she came very close to tears when May asked her in for a cup of tea and a chat. May had noticed Kate had seemed very quiet and guarded in the way she spoke about life next door, but when asked outright how things were going, Kate just managed to make a feeble excuse about having left a cake in the oven and dash out the door, not daring to look back.

Feeling as if her heart would give way, and in so many ways wishing it would, all Kate could do was to rush upstairs, collapse on the bed, and give way to the unstoppable flood of tears. Right now she felt life was not worth living, yet she knew she had to for Sarah's sake. Though she knew she was not responsible for Jack's behaviour really, she couldn't prevent a heavy weight of guilt for allowing him into their lives, and knew she must guard her daughter's innocence at whatever cost.

Meanwhile, whilst Kate was desperate to preserve Sarah's innocence, Jack had formed a plan in his mind to further his ideas to rid himself of a stepdaughter he saw as a threat to his cosy existence. Though he could stand Sam no more than he did Sarah, he made a point on the odd occasion to have a sly 'man to man' chat with him, in which he tried to suggest to the boy,

"Yer need push her a bit lad, d'ya know what I mean. She's been too pampered, it's about time she grew up and found out what life's about."

Sam took a minute to realise just what Jack was suggesting. When it registered in his mind he was horrified. He'd been brought up to treat women and girls with respect. Here was this man, not only suggesting he should take advantage of his beloved Sarah, but actually giving his permission to do so!

"I'm sorry Mr Sheppard, but I disagree with you on that. I wouldn't dream of doing any such thing, and I don' reckon you should be suggesting it either. It's disrespectful."

"Don't be soft man, ain't your pa told you that's what yer have to do to get them ta show respect to yer? Anyway, if yer ain't gonna treat me with respect you can get out my house and leave her for me to teach after I've finished with her ma."

Sam had often disagreed with things Jack had said or done during the time he'd been coming regularly to the house, but had chosen to show at least a pretence of respect, thinking that was the necessary thing to do if he hoped to woo Sarah. But this was asking too much. This was just more than Sam could take!

Before he could help himself Sam was aware of a stream of abuse being hurled at the older man, and the words were out before he could believe they were actually coming from his own mouth! He had never in his life spoken to anyone, let alone an elder that way, but neither could he believe this man would even speak of such atrocities towards his Sarah.

Just for a brief moment his outburst stopped Sheppard in his tracks, but only for the very briefest moment. Before Sam could catch his breath he found himself grabbed unceremoniously by the collar, dragged to the door, and slung out so roughly as to leave him flat on his face on the pavement outside. For a second he just remained where he'd landed before dragging himself up, dusting himself off, and turning for home.

What should he do now? He knew he must protect Sarah from the threat of what her step-father threatened…but what could he do? He knew he was no match physically for Jack but the threat seemed so real he knew he must find an answer. He'd go home and speak to his Pa, after all Pa was the one who had always told him he should treat women with respect. Yes, that's what he must do, speak to Pa.

Chapter Nineteen.

Repercussions.

When Sam arrived home shortly after his ungainly eviction from the Burgess, or was it now the Sheppard, house, Mr Hackett was emptying coal from the scuttle onto the fire and stoking it up with the poker. As soon as he looked round he could tell by his son's expression that something serious was on his mind.

"Hello lad, you're late tonight, why'd you look so worried? You're not in bother with the coppers are you?"

"No Pa, of course not. But there's something serious I need to talk to you about," Sam ventured cautiously on.
"Come on then, spit it out boy, Ma'll have tea ready before yer do at this rate."

"Well Pa, you know as how you always said it was right and proper to treat women with respect?"

Mr Hackett put down the poker and turned on his son, "This had better not be about the Burgess girl. Don't you dare tell me you've pushed your luck with her and got her in trouble? Didn't I tell you to leave her be? Why, I'll knock your bloody teeth out if…"

As he said this he marched across the room towards Sam, who was quick to step sideways to avoid his father's wrath in time to say, "No Pa, just listen to me. Please listen before you jump to conclusions."

Seeing his son was obviously upset about something Mr Hackett backed off enough to give Sam chance to explain.
"It's that Jack Sheppard Pa. He was trying to tell me I should…well you know, do things you've always said was wrong Pa, and…"

"I knew it, I knew it'd have something to do with her. Didn't I warn you to keep yer distance from that one?"

"But Pa, you've not heard the worst of it. Please just let me finish. I need your help to know what to do, how to help Sarah Pa," Sam pleaded with his father, but Mr Hackett was having none of it.

"T'aint for you to help her. She's got her ma and that Sheppard bloke to look out for her, and yer can bet whatever he said was just to wind yer up; just to make you back off like I've been telling yer, but no, yer wouldn't listen would yer?"

Not prepared to let it drop, Sam stood his ground and argued the toss with his father in his desperation to prove his intentions were good. No matter how much he tried, Mr Hackett wouldn't believe what Sam told him, wouldn't accept that it was more than

Sheppard having a laugh at Sam's expense. As a father he couldn't imagine there was any truth in it.

The more Sam tried to convince him, and the more he kept appealing for a way to help Sarah, the more his father's temper rose from annoyance to uncontrollable rage. Never had he had his son argue the toss so vehemently or sounded so defiant.

For Sam's part, he just couldn't believe how, from his point of view, Pa couldn't see that he had to be there for Sarah. She had no-one else since her Pa was dead, and he couldn't just walk away and pretend he'd not heard what Sheppard had threatened. It just wasn't right.

Both voices were raised to such a level that, within a short while, Mrs Hackett came scurrying in from the back yard where she had been hanging the washing out, wanting to see what was amiss, but it was too late. Things had come to a head and she entered the room just in time to hear her husband's explosive outburst,

"Then pack yer stuff and get out. If yer can't live by my rules yer don't belong under my roof anymore. Go on, get out!"

To which Sam replied, "That's fine by me if that's how you want it," and left the room, slamming the door behind him.

Mrs Hackett wanted to ask what caused such a row but had never seen her husband so enraged, and was more concerned with the immediate effect it had on his breathing. The effect of shouting at Sam and getting himself so wound up had brought on a drastic attack of coughing and wheezing, and this was her first priority, finding out what caused it could wait. By the time she had calmed him enough to take a few sips of water and settle enough to talk Sam had thrown his clothes in a bag and gone.

Just where he had gone no one knew, nor how he would manage, but truth be told, this was not the way either Sam or his parents had ever envisaged him leaving home, and left all concerned shaken by the whole event.

Chapter Twenty.

Sam's Effort.

The following Monday Sam was not in the usual place to meet Sarah from work. After waiting for an extra ten minutes she decided to carry on without him. By the time she arrived home Kate was all ready to dish up their meal, and was somewhat surprised to hear he didn't come.

Then, just as the family were about to sit down at the table there was a knock on the door. Kate went to see who it was and came back into the room with Sam, who was quick to apologise to Sarah for missing her earlier. His explanation was that he had been invited to move in with a work mate, and had had to drop his things off there before coming round,

"I thought I'd still have time to get there to meet you but my mate kept me talking, and I didn't like to be rude y'know."

Sarah seemed quite indifferent to whether he was there or not, whilst Kate said in her usual welcoming and motherly way, "That's no bother lad, sit yourself down, I was just about to dish up anyway."

Had either of the women taken the time to study the exchange of looks which passed between Sam and Jack Sheppard, they could most certainly not have missed the look of hate that was almost palpable, yet gone in an instant. For the rest of the meal there was nothing to distinguish this from any other occasion, in fact, later that evening as the women dealt with clearing away and washing up, they overheard Jack invite Sam for a beer in the cellar.

On this occasion Jack remembered to secure the door on their way down, and as Sarah passed it on her way to bring the remaining dishes to the kitchen, was surprised to hear quite some noise coming from behind it.

"I don't know what they're up to down there, but they seem to be doing a lot of banging about. No doubt that'll be even more mess in Father's office," she said sadly.

"All you can hope is that he doesn't get young Sam into his bad ways dear. I'm really quite fond of the boy, and believe he is quite fond of you in his way."

"Oh Mother; Sam's just a friend. He's Annie's brother, no more than that. Surely you don't think he'd be my sort of lad to take up with, do you?"

Without realising it Sarah's words were out before she saw she was being overheard. A warning glance from her mother made Sarah turn and find herself looking into Sam's face, a face bearing an expression of such deep hurt and humiliation that in that minute she could not help but understand just how badly hurt he was by what she had just said. Honestly, she had always looked upon Sam as just a good friend, and as Annie's brother. That in her mind made him almost a brother to her. But now she understood, now she could see why he was so keen to walk her home, so keen to stay for tea, in fact so much suddenly became clear in that moment.

"I...I didn't mean..." she stammered.

"That's fine," Sam jumped in to stop her before she made things even more humiliating for both of them, "you're right. We're just good friends aren't we? I just want to keep you safe, just like I would our Annie."

Before more could be said between them a loud bellow rang out from the cellar below,

"Get y'self back down here boy. I ain't finished with you yet."

Sam looked hesitantly toward the cellar door. In spite of what had just passed between them he couldn't get that man's threats out of his mind. He had been about to make his excuses, knowing that Jack had already pushed him to drink far more than he was used to, and having decided he was not ready to tackle him whilst the women were in the house, was planning to leave it for today at least.

"Are you alright down there with him Sam?" Sarah cut into his thoughts, "Don't let him bully you will you?"

At that moment her obvious concern, sisterly though it may be, shone through his hurt, reminding him of the very reason he just couldn't help loving her, even if she didn't share his feelings.

No, he knew he had to go back down there into the cellar and face him like a man, for his dear Sarah's sake. She might not want him, he thought, but she still might need his protection.

A while later Kate and Sarah sat quietly reading, they couldn't help but be aware of a great amount of noise coming again from below, followed by silence. Five minutes later the front door slammed.

As Jack passed the living room door Kate asked, "Where's Sam dear?"

"Just seen him out. Reckon he's a bit of a light-weight. Can't hold his drink like a man that one," and let out a disgusting laugh as he headed off back down for more of the same.

After that evening Sam stopped meeting Sarah, not that she was surprised after how she'd hurt his feelings so badly, but he also failed to turn up for his tea on the usual two days the following week.

Sarah felt really quite guilty and couldn't help asking Annie when they met next, was he alright? To her surprise Annie told her that she had no idea how he was. She explained that all she knew was that her mother said he'd had a blazing row with his father, packed his bag and walked out. She didn't dare ask just what it was about but just knew her mother was very worried about where he'd gone.

Though Sarah had no idea why he had argued with his father, she told Annie that he'd come for his tea as usual, stayed afterwards and had a couple of drinks (she thought probably a few more than a couple), before leaving without saying goodbye. That in itself seemed strange at the time but, as she admitted to his sister, she thinks Jack must have plied him with enough to make him just want to go home.

"That's the point though, that's what's worrying Ma," Annie explained, "He'd left earlier, before work, and never come home."

"Well, you see, he didn't meet me as he usually did. Just turned up as Mother was about to dish up. Then he told us that was because he'd decided to move out of home and in with one of his mates from work. No doubt that's where he went."

Annie asked if Sarah knew the name of the mate he'd gone to stay with, but unfortunately it had not occurred to Sarah to ask that. They agreed that it would probably be just a matter of time before Sam returned home and made things up with his father. Sarah promised to question him as to where he was staying the next time he came for his tea, and to let Annie know.

But for whatever reason, Sam stopped coming altogether.

Chapter Twenty-One

Kate's Concern.

As the weeks went on Kate continued to suffer the pain and humiliation Jack put her through. Whenever possible she tried to avoid him if she knew he'd been drinking, which was much of the time. She also worked hard at finding reasons to keep Sarah out of his way for fear he might take advantage of her too. For the first time in her daughter's life, Kate began to wish she could suggest she moved out, or at the very least found employment which kept her out of the house more.

It was about this time that Jack, beginning to tire of his wife did, as Kate had dreaded might happen, start to turn his attention to Sarah. For a long time Kate was unaware of this.

At first he would brush past Sarah a bit too closely when they passed in the hall. Then he would put an arm around her in a false show of fatherly affection which had the effect of making her shudder at his touch.

One night when he had been drinking and Kate was asleep he crept into Sarah's bedroom whilst she was asleep and surreptitiously slipped between the sheets. She awoke suddenly to the feel of his rough hand slide across her and instinctively went to let out a frightened scream. This was quickly stifled by one strong hand whilst the other continued on its terrifying journey around her lithe young body. Sarah froze with fear, not knowing what to do to stop him, her only instinct telling her to scream for help, yet unable to do so. Even the smell of his drink ridden breath repulsed her to the point of making her retch. Sarah had never felt so repulsed or so scared in her young life, and it was as if her fear just acted as a means of more pleasure for him, leaving her with absolutely no defence against him.

"Not a word to mother," he warned her before he left, "you wouldn't want to upset her now, would you dear," he leered at her. Of course she wouldn't. Nor would she know how to speak of this nightmare to anyone else and of this he was well aware.

Though Sarah originally hoped this would be just the one such happening this was not to be. Now that he had realised the extra pleasure he could get from the younger body of his step-daughter there was little chance of stopping him. Therefore the cycle continued; drinking, gambling, more drinking, followed by the frequent unwanted assaults on either his wife or step-daughter! At least, for whatever reason, he stopped short of anything worse than an embarrassing and uncomfortable grope around with Sarah, unlike his treatment of poor Kate, but this made the whole thing no less terrifying for one so young.

Even so, Kate soon became aware of her husband's sly visits to her daughter's room (not least because he left her alone on such nights), and it was at this point that she decided that it would be safer to find Sarah some form of live-in employment which would help to keep her safe from him.

By coincidence a perfect solution was to arise. On Kate's visit to the local market one morning she met up with Mrs Betts, John Lawes cook, also out collecting food for the household. During the course of their conversation it came to light that 'young Patty' the housemaid was about to leave her position to marry her young man. Mr Lawes would be in need of a replacement Mrs Betts told Kate.

"Would she need very much experience in that type of work," asked Kate.

"Not as long as she is reliable and can organise herself without much supervision, and I could soon show her the ropes in that respect. He did try getting Patty to help on once or twice to sort some paperwork for him when he was busy, but she just couldn't grasp that at all, and made a right mess of it! Took him days to sort the mess she'd made," replied the cook with a chuckle.

"That wouldn't worry Sarah, she used to help her father with his from quite an early age, and the housework is no more than she's been helping me with for years," Kate told her. "Do you think she might suit the position?"

"I reckon she'd be grand, and she's a clever one your Sarah. She'd soon get the hang of what's what. Send her over one evening and I'll get Master John to speak to her."

When she returned home and had chance to speak to Sarah she decided it would be best to avoid her real reason for the suggestion she was to make. She was quite right but, Sarah being the intelligent girl she was, the question was soon put as to why she should want to change jobs.

"Well I know you were never completely happy doing factory work, and Mrs Betts did say that Mr Lawes is keen to find someone with a little more intelligence than the average housemaid as it may entail helping with a little basic paperwork from time to time."

It was quickly arranged for Sarah to go for an interview, if such was necessary, in the hope of taking up her new post in the Lawes household within the next few days. She was to live in during the week, going home for each weekend, an arrangement that suited her well as it meant she was never too far away, or for too long, to keep a watchful eye over mother. She was still rather worried about not being there for her mother on weekday evenings but she'd be there at the weekends, and Mother could visit her should she feel the need during the week.

Perhaps, she thought, it seemed selfish to leave Mother to Jack's mercy, but she really felt she couldn't take his ever more menacing attention much longer. This, she hoped, just may be the escape she so desperately longed for.

As for Kate this was the perfect solution. Not only did it answer her concerns about her daughter wasting her life away working in a factory after all the effort dear Tom had put into her education, but most important of all, it kept Sarah away from this brute she was married to. She could, or at least would, find a way to tolerate her lot, as long as dear Sarah was safe.

Chapter Twenty-Two.

Sarah's Satisfaction.

The following Friday when Sarah got home from the factory her mother went with her to John Lawes house for an interview with him. Mrs Betts immediately made her feel welcome, showing her around and giving her an idea of the sort of jobs she would be expected to do. They had been there for around half an hour when John Lawes arrived home from his office.

Sarah felt somewhat awkward at first, knowing she must look on him as her future employer, yet finding it hard to prevent herself from greeting him like the lodger she had felt so at ease with before. For a start she wasn't sure how to address him. Of course Mrs Betts called him Master John, but that was because she had done so since he was a small boy. Though in her mind she thought of him as John, that wouldn't be appropriate either.

As Mrs Betts met him in the hall she heard her say, "Young Sarah is here to see you Master John."

Sarah stood up to meet him and, as he came into the room, found herself experiencing a feeling the like of which she had not felt before, a sort of tingling, running through her!

"Good evening Mr. Lawes," she managed to shake out the words.

"Mr Lawes is it?" he said with a slight frown, "Whatever happened to 'John'? I thought we were friends."

Noticing the slightly worried expression on her face he was quick to follow this up by flashing a genuinely felt smile in the direction of both Kate and Sarah.

"It's so good to see you both, are you keeping well ladies?"

Sarah found herself quite taken aback. This was not what she had expected, this was much more than she could have wished for. Somehow this greeting had the effect of taking her back to happier times; blocking out, for now at least, all the misery she had been living with for so long now.

They were ushered into the living room where Mrs Betts brought a tray of tea and home-made fruit cake to sustain them while they chatted. By the time they had gone over the duties that would be expected of Sarah, it was time to leave.

"I'm sure we'll get along splendidly, won't we Sarah?" he assured Kate, who by then needed no further reassurance on that score. It had not escaped her notice just how easy Sarah found it to talk to John Lawes, just how relaxed she had become during the time they sat there.

That night Kate prayed that at least her daughter was now safe.

Over the weekend she helped Sarah sort out what to take and what to leave, after all this was still her home, even if she had to be away from it for much of the time.

When Monday morning came Kate hugged her daughter and wished her luck as she picked up her bag and set off for the Lawes house. Neither had said a word of Sarah's change of situation to Jack yet. Both knew it wouldn't please him. Both were right to think that. When he came home that evening and condescended to come to the table to eat, Kate told him the news.

"I'm the head of this bloody family ain't I? And you didn't see fit to tell me what you were up to behind my back," he raged at Kate.

Kate, for once, derived great pleasure from knowing they had outfoxed him this time. Once again his food ended up on the floor. Once again she had to cope with the physical ordeal he thrust upon her later after his session in the cellar. But Kate didn't care, she had the satisfaction of knowing her daughter was safe during the week, and when she came home it would be weekends, and when he was off work at weekends, if he did stay home, he was usually too drunk to stand let alone bother with Sarah.

Meanwhile the situation in the Lawes house turned out to be so much more interesting and rewarding due to the unexpected variations to the things Sarah was asked to do. Apart from keeping the house to a reasonable standard of cleanliness, she was often called upon to sort paperwork and file it away in order. Good business man that he was Mr Lawes was obviously not so good at keeping his desk tidy and work filed in the appropriate place, and would often have to ask Sarah's help in finding a particular document…even finding his desk under these! Most of the time John Lawes worked in his office in the factory, but when the noise around him was too great to concentrate he would pack up and bring a fair proportion of his work home much, Sarah thought, as did her father, Tom Burgess.

It was on these occasions that he quickly came to realise the extent of this young lady's knowledge of such things. He had always been a fairly reclusive man, much of which was due to his upbringing, and as a consequence was used to spending much of the time in his own company. Even with his wife he had found it difficult to feel as close as he felt he should. Yet here he was feeling that he was able to open up and talk to young Sarah. Why, he wondered should that be? Perhaps because she shared his love and understanding of business matters to a certain degree. Perhaps because she somehow had an air of independence about her that his wife had never had. He had loved his wife dearly and had been so desperate for the arrival of their child, but when he lost both together, this had convinced him he would never again want anyone else in his life and, just as his father had done, had thrown everything into his work with the exclusion of all else.

As for Sarah, she thoroughly enjoyed her new employment right from the first day. Not only could she honestly say she enjoyed the variety each day, but she felt happier and more relaxed than she had done for some time. Mrs Betts was a little concerned that she might find the daily grind of housework a bit hard to deal with, but Sarah was quick to assure her that she was used to helping her mother at home, especially in the days when they took in the odd lodger.

'Lodger', the thought brought her mind back to the reality of the nightmare that was there in the background at home. She had never spoken to mother about what had happened, what she was still desperately trying to avoid on her weekends at home. At least the fact that she was out of the house on weekday evenings, and mother had found herself a small cleaning job which kept her out for a couple of nights a week, meant that on those occasions Sheppard had no choice but to drink himself into oblivion, thus rendering himself unconscious and therefore harmless to either. Of course neither had Kate even hinted to her daughter of the true extent of what she was having to live with. Both had kept the true horror of all of this away from the other, ashamed of what the other would think. Both had kept it, as it were, behind the closed doors of their minds.

Chapter Twenty-Three.

Mixed feelings for the Hackett's.

Sarah still made regular visits to the Hackett's, after all, they had almost been like a second family to her over the years. On occasions Annie and Sarah would go into town and savour the delights on at the Electric Cinema. Other times they enjoyed roaming around assorted galleries and museums of which there were plenty. But as with most of their age, what they really enjoyed was to attend local dances.

Kate never minded her daughter going out on weekend evenings as, once again, it kept her out of Jack's reach. After all, she thought, it might also encourage Sarah to pick up with some nice young man who would whisk her away for good. She would be sad to lose her but, as every mother knows, every daughter really needs a husband sooner or later!

There were a few lads who Sarah quite liked, ones she would agree to allow her on occasions to walk her to the bus stop, but somehow she couldn't seem to feel altogether safe enough to allow them to get any more familiar than a quick peck on the cheek as she saw the bus coming. Perhaps, she wondered, she was still feeling guilty from the way she'd caused such problems for poor Sam. She must have hurt him so badly; since the day he walked out of her house nobody had heard a word from him, not even Annie.

Even so, knowing now of him having had what appears to have been a massive row with Mr Hackett, he must have had a stronger reason for going off as he did. It seems from all accounts that he had also left his job without giving notice, so must have moved away altogether. Perhaps he'd took it into his head to seek his fortune in London even!

But for whatever reason, Sarah seemed unwilling or unable to form any really close attachment to any of the young men who tried so hard to gain favour with her. In fact, it seemed to Kate that, the more they tried to endear themselves to her, the further away she pushed them. Was this that she genuinely couldn't find the right one, or was it as a result of Jack's unwanted attentions, Kate wondered?

On the other hand Annie had been meeting up with a very nice young chap by the name of Charlie Potts. They had been meeting up at the dances most Saturdays now for some time. After a while she had taken home to meet her parents and the other children. To her great relief both Mr and Mrs Hackett had taken to him from the start.

"I reckon our Annie's picked a real good'n there ain't she," Mrs Hackett commented to her husband following Charlie's visit one day.

"You're right there. Why our Sam couldn't have just waited a while and found someone more suitable, like our Annie's done, I don't know. He'd probably not have gone off like he did. "

What neither of them knew was that Annie was just passing the door at that moment and, on hearing what was said, came straight in to confront them on the subject of what she'd overheard,

"What do you mean, what really happened with Sam? Why did he go Pa?" Annie was not going to be fobbed off any more. She dearly missed her brother but had never been told just what had been the cause of the argument between him and their father. Reluctantly she was at last told of his fancy for Sarah and how Pa had tried to tell him she wasn't right for him. Her mother was quick to explain that they'd not meant anything against Sarah, just that they felt she was a little out of his class when it came to taking things further than just friendship.

Annie felt rather torn now between her brother and her best friend, her almost sister. Should she say anything about this to Sarah? She didn't want to upset her or lose her friendship, but wondered if Sarah ever knew this is why he left? When she did put it to Sarah later that week it was clear that Sarah was genuinely shocked to think she had been the cause of Sam's row with his father. As she explained to Annie, she knew she hurt his feelings the last time she saw him, but had never considered that to be anything to do with him leaving home.

"I wish we could find him though," Annie told her, "cos' I think Charlie is going to propose to me, I overheard him speaking to Pa last night, and I'd love to have Sam there with me when we wed."

Of course Annie was right. The next night on the way home from the cinema, Charlie did propose and, trying hard to look surprised, Annie threw herself into his arms hardly before he'd finished getting the words from his mouth. In spite of her plan to be dignified and act surprised she felt completely overwhelmed with the joy of the moment.

This was on the Saturday night, and so consequently Annie rushed straight round to tell Sarah the good news the next morning, unable to contain her excitement a moment longer.

"That's brilliant news Annie, I'm so pleased for you," Sarah told her as they hugged one another.

"And of course you will be my bridesmaid won't you? I've already got some good ideas for our dresses, and Ma and me'll make them up, so it won't cost too much. Please say yes," she pleaded with Sarah.

"Are you sure you want me to, after the trouble I've caused over Sam?"

Annie was quick to reassure her that she didn't hold her responsible for what happened with Sam, explaining that she thought he was probably of an age to make his own way in the world by now, and must just have been put out by his father accusing him of only being a boy, so just as likely had gone off to prove he was man enough to manage alone.

Unknown to Annie, Sarah determined to visit Sam's previous place of work to ask those Sam had worked with if any had heard from him. None had. All they could do was to promise to tell him about his sister's wedding and ask him, please, to come home for this if any should hear from him. When Sarah found herself relaying the sad tale of Sam's disappearance to John Lawes one afternoon as she was helping him sort some files into proper order, he listened intently. After a little thought he asked,

"Has anyone considered reporting him to the police as a missing person?"

"Oh no! They wouldn't like that idea. Mr Hackett wouldn't stand for that. He's a very proud man, and would hate anyone outside the family to know their business."

Sarah felt she'd upset the family enough already without going behind their backs, and so the search came to an end. Consequently the weeks between this conversation and the wedding were taken up in the Hackett household with planning, dressmaking, and last of all, the rehearsal in the little church near their home, leaving them with a mix of emotions from deepest sadness at missing Sam, and extreme happiness at the upcoming nuptials of their eldest daughter.

Chapter Twenty-Four.

Mixed Emotions.

By this time Sarah had been fully ensconced in her new employment with John Lawes. She still found it difficult to address him as John, indeed often reverted to Mr Lawes, which would often cause him to tut at her and throw a grin in her direction (the effect of which was more often than not to send that same tingle through her as on the first time!).

The work she was asked to do made her feel so much more fulfilled than any she'd done previously. The more her employer realised just how much she had to offer thanks to the time she had spent with her father, the more he made use of this and sneaked her out from the grasp of Mrs Betts as often as possible to help him with his company books and papers. In fact he found it quite amusing on occasions when he would lose concentration out of sheer boredom, just to find that Sarah would be the one to steer him, quite politely, back onto the straight line of whatever it was they'd be working on.

When meeting up with Kate at the market one day, Mrs Betts was pleased to report that she felt young Sarah was fitting in well.

"I've often taken tea in for them when I thought they were hard at it doing accounts or some such, just to find him regaling her with stories of his travels, and her sat mesmerised!"

"You've no idea how much that means to know she's happy at last. She's not been truly happy since poor Tom died. Come to that, neither have I. I'm just so grateful to you for finding her that situation, and making it possible for her to stay away all week."

Mrs Betts threw Kate a suspicious look before asking, "Kate, just what's going on with your Jack? You said before about his short temper but not said more than that. You do know if he's getting out of hand you should go to the police and report him don't you?"

"Stop worrying about me Mrs Betts, I can look after myself, it was Sarah I was more concerned with."

More than that Kate felt unable to put into words, but Mrs Betts knew enough of the ways of Jack's like to form a pretty good idea, and wished she could do more to help. All she could do was to be a good friend to Kate, and help keep Sarah away from home during the week. From that day on, Mrs Betts made a point of visiting Kate from time to time, hoping to see just how he was treating Kate, and though he worked hard at disguising his worst tendencies when she was there, she could always tell that behind closed doors, he would have no qualms in how badly he'd behave towards poor Kate. She knew Kate was just too proud a person to speak of what she'd consider unspeakable, leaving it clear meanwhile that the best thing to do was to keep young Sarah tucked safely under her wing.

On one occasion Mrs Betts invited Kate to return with her to the Lawes house as it began to rain whilst they were chatting on the corner of the market square, and it was closer than Kate's house. As they sat sharing a cup of tea in the kitchen there was the sound of laughter from the study.

"That's your Sarah being told more of Master John's stories I'll wager."

Kate listened incredulously. She honestly couldn't remember when she'd last heard her dear Sarah sound so happy. The sound of her laughter gave Kate such pleasure and such satisfaction in knowing this was the best thing she could have done for her. But why, oh why, couldn't she be this happy in her own home…the answer was obvious, Jack Sheppard!

The following evening Annie arrived carrying a carefully wrapped parcel. Sarah was just finishing off some filing with John in the study when Mrs Betts popped her head round the door to tell her.

"I think Annie has come to let me try the bridesmaid dress her mother was just finishing," she told John.

"Right," he said immediately, "off you go, don't keep her waiting. Please will you show me? From what you've told me your Mrs Hackett is pretty handy with a needle."

"I'll see what Annie says," replied Sarah replied as she left the room.

A short while after Sarah tapped on the door and came back in, accompanied by Annie, and wearing a dress of such a stunning blue that all John could see was how it emphasised the colour of her eyes.

"Well, what do you think then? Do you think I'll look alright Mr...er, John?"

Not being quite able to put his thoughts into words, well, not any he should be using to a young lady of her age anyway, just for a second he had to collect himself together, remember the age gap between them, before saying,

"Yes Sarah, I think that dress is beautiful," and turning to Annie added, "If that's the dress you've made for your bridesmaid, yours must be stunning Miss Hackett, or may I call you Annie?"

"Thank you Sir, that's good of you to say, and yes, of course I'd be honoured for you to call me Annie."

This was the first time Annie had met John Lawes, but could see immediately just why Sarah felt so happy to be in his company. He did have a remarkable way of putting you at your ease, even for the likes of her, coming from a very much more humble background than his.

That weekend Sarah went home as usual. She chose to leave her beautiful blue dress hanging in the wardrobe in her room at work, feeling that it would be somehow safer there. All week she'd looked at it hanging there and couldn't wait for the day of the wedding so that she would get to wear it again. As John had suggested, Annie's dress was even more stunning, made of ivory silk, decorated with beading, and finished off with a veil to match, all so carefully made by her mother.

Sarah couldn't wait to describe both to Kate that evening while they were clearing the table. Kate listened intently and shared her daughter's enthusiasm at the idea of being Annie's bridesmaid. Jack, on the other hand was quick to scorn the whole idea saying,

"Ain't it time you were a bride, never mind bridesmaid. What's up with yer that makes lads go for the like of her but want nowt to do with you?"

"That's not fair Jack," Kate jumped in without hesitation to defend her daughter, "What chance has she got when you think how you treated poor Sam? You put him off so much he's left home…"

But before she could go on Jack's temper took over and he lashed out, hitting her across the face so hard Sarah stepped in to catch her before she could fall.

"I hate you, you nasty, cowardly drunk, leave my mother alone."
For a second Sarah thought he was going to hit her too. For that second he thought to do so; but in the end he just swore at them, threw yet another plate, kicked over Kate's sewing box which had

been by the side of her chair, and stormed out of the house for what they guessed would be another night of drinking!

Though both had survived his wrath this time, Kate knew that, even worse than this new bruise that was already forming on the side of her face, the pain yet to come that night would not be so easy to bear. But bear it she must, for Sarah's sake. She knew if she made any attempt to refuse him he might turn to Sarah instead.

When he did finally roll in that night he was in a particularly awful state. It was all he could do to climb the stairs, but when he did Kate laid, gritting her teeth waiting, expecting at any moment to see him barge in the bedroom door, do his worst, and then collapse unconscious on the bed until morning.

As she waited she realised it was not her door that he was opening…it was Sarah's! Without hesitation Kate leapt up, not sure what she could do to stop him, but determined to try.

She needn't have worried after all; it seemed Sarah had also guessed at the consequences of her earlier verbal attack on him. Try as he might, especially in his drunken state, she had had the forethought to barricade the door from the inside by pushing her chest of drawers in front of it. Under normal circumstances this would not have been heavy enough to stop him, but in his present condition he was much weakened by drink.

That night at least, Sarah felt she was safe. By the time she returned to John's house on the Monday morning Sarah looked back over the last week with very mixed emotions. She'd gone from contentment with her employment, to the joy of helping

Annie, to sheer excitement at the sight of her beautiful new dress, yet ended up the week with such horror dished out by Jack Sheppard.

Chapter Twenty-Five.

Annie's Wedding.

Eventually the big day arrived. It was Annie and Charlie's wedding day. Though it wasn't to be a huge affaire, Mr and Mrs Hackett knew that eventually there would come a time to have to pay for weddings for Susie and Mary, being such a popular family in the area, the whole community had pulled together to help make it a really memorable affair.

Obviously it had been Mrs Hackett, helped by Annie herself, who had made the dresses for Sarah, Susie and Mary. Much of the food for the wedding breakfast was supplied from the allotments of assorted friends and cooked by various people including Kate. But the real pièce de résistance as far as food was concerned was a surprise given by Mrs Betts of a particularly grand cake.

Since she'd got to know Annie from her visits to see Sarah at her place of work, she had taken a real shine to the girl. Without mentioning this to Annie she had taken it upon herself to call on Mrs Hackett one day and offer to make the cake as a wedding present from both herself and her employer, John Lawes.

Of course Mr Hackett had to be persuaded, being an extremely proud man, that this was not in any way charity, just a friendly gesture by a lovely lady who was genuinely fond of his daughter, and of course cooking being her lifetimes occupation, she was well qualified to make it.

Knowing that John Lawes had been happy for the ingredients for the cake to come from his kitchen, and for him to allow his cook to prepare it, Mrs Hackett had, with some trepidation, told Annie to offer him an invitation to the wedding. To her surprise and delight he accepted without hesitation. What nobody could possibly know of course was just how much it meant to him to be included into such a close community after feeling such an outsider for much of his life. He'd always felt as a child he was never good enough. In fact the only time he had begun to feel he fitted in was just for the short time he'd been in South Africa and married to his wife, but the devastation of the loss he suffered with her death had put him right back into what could only be described as his protective shell. Wanting so badly to be a part of society, yet scared to open himself up to the risk of even more loss.

Now, having young Sarah around to help bring a sense of lightness and normality into the house, things were changing. When Mrs Betts asked him if she might make the wedding cake, he had no hesitation in giving his approval. What he did not expect was that he would actually be invited to attend.

"Thank you Annie," he said, "but are you really sure your parents won't mind? After all, nobody there knows me, and I don't want to intrude."

Annie had been quick to assure him that her parents had particularly asked that he come, and so, on the day he escorted Mrs Betts to the church. Though he had doubted the welcome he might get from the family and friends of the bride and groom, he was soon put at ease by everyone he met.

He'd not been in his seat at the end of the pew many minutes when the organ struck up with the wedding march, so, like the whole congregation, he immediately turned toward the door to see Annie enter in her beautiful cream silk dress on the arm of her proud father. She really did look amazing and the picture of happiness. She was followed down the aisle of the little church by her two sisters and Sarah.

Sarah? Is that really our Sarah? He couldn't believe this was the same young girl he'd lodged with before, that same young girl who spent so much time in his house working alongside him! This was no young girl…this was a beautiful young woman. Why had not noticed her growing up so much in the time he had known her.

Just then Mrs Betts gave him a sharp poke, just as she may have done to get his attention as a young boy. This brought him back to reality in time to realise the congregation were already in full voice with the first hymn. Reminding himself of his position as a guest of the Hackett's, and as Sarah's employer, he pulled himself together and enjoyed the rest of the proceedings.

After the service everybody was ushered round to the small church hall behind to sample the delights the ladies had worked so hard to produce. Charlie got to his feet to make a speech, but found himself so tongue tied in the attempt that his brother and best man, Bert came to his rescue, reducing everyone to fits of laughter with some of the rather hilarious tales of things Charlie had done over the years!

After the cake was cut, shame though Annie thought to do so as she'd never had the likes before, the tables were cleared away and dancing took over. Annie and Charlie were first to take to the floor, but then gradually nearly all took a turn around the floor, even Kate who, needless to say had had to attend without her husband as he was, as she explained apologetically to Mr and Mrs Hackett, not comfortable with such gatherings, but had, she lied, sent his very best wishes for the happy couple. Therefore she was more than pleased to find John Lawes, who was still feeling a little like a fish out of water amongst so many who were clearly good friends of the family, was pleased to ask her to join him on the dance floor.

Sarah found the sight of her mother having such an enjoyable time so comforting. She knew by now much of the hardship and misery Jack was putting on her. Poor Mother had never recovered from the loss of dear Father, she thought. Now, instead of the true happiness they had shared Mother was suffering at the hands of that cruel, evil creature who could never be half the man her father had been!

After a while Sarah found herself sitting with the two younger bridesmaids, Susie and Mary, discussing what a special experience it had been to hold such important positions for Annie, when she was aware of a light tap on the shoulder. She immediately looked round and was somewhat surprised to find John Lawes looking down at her with a smile on his face which made her, just for that moment, forget he was her employer.

"May I have the pleasure of this dance Sarah? I feel you've been sitting down for far too long, and if I don't ask now I'm afraid there'll be a long line of young men queuing up, and I won't get another opportunity."

She doubted that, but gave him her hand, and as he walked her to the dance floor and took his hold of her, once again she was aware of that same sensation she'd had a few times before. After that, had anyone asked, she would have to have admitted that she was unaware of anyone or anything around them, just that for that few minutes her world was completely encircled by his arms.

Chapter Twenty-Six.

Revelations.

After the wedding celebrations were at an end Kate, with great reluctance, agreed to allow John to escort both her and Sarah home. First, while they stayed on to help Mrs Hackett clear up the mess left behind from that amazing feast, he took Mrs Betts home, before returning for Kate and Sarah. Truth be known, he had picked up suspicions from conversations he'd overheard between Mrs Betts and Kate, suspicions which made him feel uncomfortable. This was a chance to get the lie of the land in what used to be the Burgess household.

He'd guessed things were not exactly as they should be but, when they were met at the door by this man who was obviously drunk and extremely abusive, John was genuinely quite shocked.

"Where the 'ell a yer been all this time? I ain't had nothing to eat," and then looking at John, "and what d'you want eh?"

Standing his ground, John looked him straight in the eye, unable to hide his feeling of disgust at this excuse for a man, and simply said,

"I don't *want* anything. I'm just doing my duty and escorting the ladies home, as I'm sure you would sir."

"I'm sure I wouldn't *sir*," Sheppard sneered back at him, "and as for ladies …these ain't no ladies. Now scram before I flatten you!"

"Please leave Mr Lawes, it would be best if you do, but thank you for seeing us home safely," Kate suggested, not wishing to see things escalate between the two of them.

Later that evening as he sat deep in thought, Mrs Betts popped in to see if there was anything else he'd be needing.

"Not really thank you Mrs Betts," and then just as she turned to leave the room, "but perhaps you'd care to join me for a nightcap and a chat before you retire? I would appreciate your opinion on certain things."

"That would be very agreeable Master John, thank you."

John poured her a glass of sherry and a brandy for himself and sat back down wearing a worried expression wondering just where to start. He needn't have worried as, knowing he'd escorted Kate and Sarah home, she already had her suspicions as to the reception he would have received from Jack Sheppard.

"You've met him then?" she interceded into his obvious difficulty in finding the words he needed.

He looked up at her, grateful to find she could still read his mind in the way she had always since he was a boy. "Obviously you have too, and how did you find him?"

"A vile, bad tempered bully and a drunk! Wouldn't trust him as far as I could throw him," was her unhesitating answer.

"And how do think he treats Sarah and her Mother? Surely he can't be like that all the time?"

"Between you and me Master John, I believe he makes their lives hell. It was to get young Sarah out of his reach that Kate was so keen she should come here to work. God know just what poor Kate has to suffer at his hands when she's alone with him and he … oh, sorry, I really shouldn't say, it's not my place."

"Oh God Mrs Betts, you don't mean he, well …"

"Yes Master John, that's exactly what I do mean, but Kate is too proud, or perhaps too scared, to report him. As she says, he's her husband so they'd probably do nothing. Then heaven knows what he'd do to her!"

"There must be something we can do. For Sarah's sake he must be stopped."

It came clear to Mrs Betts as they talked that John was extremely fond of Sarah. More so perhaps than the usual employer employee relationship. She finally went off to bed that night with very mixed feelings. He was obviously keen to protect Sarah from her stepfather, but she also knew he had plans to travel back to South Africa to carry on the work he'd started there. The factory here was, after all, running smoothly under the control of his deputy manager and could be left to continue that way.

So far only she knew of this plan due to him discussing the idea of retiring her when the time came with a good annuity to see her through for life. Sarah meanwhile had not been warned of this. Just how he could help her Mrs Betts had no idea.

She needn't have worried about this. John already had an idea in mind, one he hoped upon hope might prove one Sarah would consider. Just how and when to face her with this he would need to think about.

<u>Chapter Twenty-Seven.</u>

<u>Decisions.</u>

Sarah sat alone in her room at home, so many thoughts racing through her head, so much confusion, so many decisions ...what should she do?

It was towards the middle of 1921 and Sarah, who was now just coming up to twenty-one years old, had been working at the Lawes household for nearly a year now. Now once again things were about to change in her life. The big question was, just what those changes were to be. The obvious change was that she was about to find herself unemployed and for a while at least, possibly spending more time at home and at the mercy of Jack Sheppard.

Yet there now presented a possibility of a different change altogether, one she had never, could never, have contemplated. The fact was that for some months now Mr. Lawes had been preparing to emigrate to live in South Africa to pursue his business interests and three weeks ago had asked her to accompany him there, not as his housemaid, but as his wife!

Should she go? She had secretly been fond of him from the start. She knew that on his part at least this must be a marriage of convenience (he was after all fourteen years her senior), as he would need a wife to set up and run a new home and entertain business colleagues. Still, she believed him when he assured her of his genuine fondness for her, yet as he had never made the slightest attempt to make any advances she had no way of judging to what depth his feelings may go.

Also in the back of her mind she couldn't help wondering, after her treatment at her step-father's hands, just how she would react if he did make those advances? She felt she would never know the answer to this question until it was too late. Even so, at present she had always felt completely safe around him, in fact, save shaking her hand the very first time he came to her mother's house, he had not laid one finger on her, but would she ever be able to be a proper wife to him, and how would he react if she found she could not?

Sarah wondered what it would be like to be a wife to this quiet, slightly distant man, who had after all, been married once before? He had said he would be proud to make her his wife and promised her happiness, but *could* she earn his pride - and *would* she be happy? And what, she wondered, would life be like in this strange, remote land she had only read about in books? It would be too far to just 'pop back' if she was homesick. Too far from home if she found herself missing … missing what? What was there to miss? Mother of course. Poor mother. Would she, could she, leave her to the mercy of *him*?

Though all these thoughts and worries had gone round and round inside her head for three weeks now, the time never seemed right to unburden her mind to her mother, and it was almost too late to matter now as Mr Lawes was due to leave in just over a weeks' time. Even so, he had entreated her to reconsider what he assumed was her decision not to go just that day, and she had promised to do so.

As Sarah sat pondering all these conflicting thoughts in her head she was suddenly aware of a gentle hand on her shoulder and the familiar, soothing voice of her mother entered her consciousness,

"What's troubling you dear?"

Kate, showing her usual intuitive understanding of Sarah's mood on her return from work that day had followed her to her room. Sarah hesitated, but Kate sat down alongside of her on the bed and put a coaxing hand on her daughter's shoulder. That was all it needed to release the full flow of Sarah's internal torment. It cascaded out like water from a ruptured dam and, once released, Sarah felt powerless to control her voice or her emotions. All the hurt she had suffered so silently for so long came to the surface and could not be kept from escaping.

She had never wanted to burden Kate with any of this but the sheer relief of letting go overcame her and, before she could stop herself, the news of Mr. Lawes proposal had reached the incredulous ears of her mother. Barely flinching at the quickly realised prospect of losing her beloved daughter forever, Kate smiled lovingly at Sarah's tear-drenched face, and asked simply,

"Do you love him my dear?"

"Well, I do feel happy when I'm with him, and he gives me such a feeling of warmth and safety. Often lately he has asked me to sit with him and talk - you wouldn't believe the things we talk about - he knows so much, and he makes me laugh, and .... and yes, I really think I do love him. Is that wrong?"

Somehow it seemed wrong to Sarah to admit to such feelings of happiness, knowing how miserable her mother's life had been lately. Kate on the other hand felt a great wave of relief sweep over her at what appeared to her to be the answer to her prayers to protect her daughter from further torment. Kate threw her arms around her daughter, and laughed,

"No dear, oh no, it's not wrong at all, it's very, very right! I'm so pleased for you and, of course you must go. Go and make a new life for yourself. I realise there is a big difference in your ages but I know John Lawes well enough to know that he wouldn't have asked if he had the slightest doubt in his mind. Though I will miss you so much I can't think of anyone kinder or more trustworthy than him to take you away from all this," Kate shot a glance over her shoulder in the direction of the sound of a deafening thud on the stairs, followed by a rush of drunken oaths pouring from the mouth of her husband, "Get away from *him* for good."

John Lawes was so pleased the next day to hear that she was to agree to his proposal. He had no objections either to postponing the wedding until her coming of age, which would be towards the end of their voyage, as Sarah told him at her mother's suggestion that this would save the difficult task of seeking her step-fathers consent. He had always been aware that Sarah didn't get on with that man but, though he had his suspicions, he had never dared enquire into the exact reasons though, since meeting the man and the conversation with Mrs Betts, could only hope he could whisk her away before any further damage could be done to her. She was truthful in assuring him that her mother had given her blessing to the match, and that seemed to mean a lot to him.

Chapter Twenty-Eight.

Preparations and the Pain.

That week seemed to Sarah to pass by in a whirl of activity. John, as he insisted she must accustom herself to calling him now, dashed about organising a passport and the appropriate tickets for the journey, whilst she helped Mrs Betts with the job of packing up his things and preparing the house for the new occupant. This was to be the new manager of John's business interests there in Birmingham, and Mrs Betts was to stay on for as long as she felt able to remain in what had been her home for so long.

The following weekend Sarah went home to pack the last of her few belongings and to say a reluctant farewell to her mother. Between the two women the rather sparse amount of luggage was soon packed and made ready to go, amongst this a small framed photo of Sarah's father, Tom Burgess. Kate was keen for Sarah to have this remembrance of him to remind her of happier times. They made a point of doing this as much as possible during the afternoon when Jack was out, supposedly at work, and when they heard him return they discreetly finished off very quietly while he was in the cellar and hid the bags inside the wardrobe lest he should venture near her room.

Once again a large part of the meal Kate had prepared for him had been rudely rejected in favour of yet another trip to the pub. This gave mother and daughter their last few hours together, time to share the deep and close affection they had always felt and would always feel for each other, no matter by what or how far they were separated . It was early evening, just getting dusk, when Kate, struggling to put on a brave face, said to Sarah,

"I think you should go now dear, while he is out and won't see you leave. Now, have you got everything you need? I'll really miss you my love, but we can keep in touch by post. I would love to hear all about your journey, your new home, and most of all of course you must send me photos of your wedding."

"I do really wish you could be with me that day. Of course I'll send photos, but it won't be the same as having you by my side." Sarah looked so crestfallen at this thought.

Kate reassured her with a warm, motherly hug and a reminder of why she must leave and not look back.

"Now come along my darling girl, let me see that wonderful smile of yours once more before you leave, then off you go before he catches you, and try to forget he ever existed; just remember the good times. Remember the life we had when your father was here and be as happy in your life with John as I was with your father."

So intense had been their last few moments together that neither had heard the tell-tale footsteps on the stairs announcing Jack Sheppard's return from his usual haunt of the local public house. There was a roar of anger from the doorway,

"What the 'ell's going on 'ere? You ain't going nowhere girl. I ain't done with you yet,"

They turned to see Jack, bottle in hand lunge towards them. For a split second they both froze at the shock of his violent attack, but then instinctively Kate stepped forward to shield Sarah. There was a sickening thud as the bottle came down on Kate's head and she fell lifeless to the floor at his feet.

With a scream of terror Sarah rushed towards her mother,
"No, Oh God no," she cried, "You brute, you murderer. You've killed her."

"Maybe I have," growled Sheppard, "And if you think you're leaving this house, you can think again. I'll kill you too before I'll let you go anywhere with that bloody man..."

His last words were inaudible by now, partly due to his drunken slurring, and partly due to the door being slammed as he left the room. The key turned in the lock and Sarah was aware of him swearing as he slipped again on the stairs.

Sarah sat cradling Kate's head in her lap and wept. It was some time later before she was in a fit state to consider her plight. The locked door was no problem. Father had never liked the bedroom doors locked therefore none of them really worked properly.

Fearfully she crept quietly downstairs, not sure what she should expect to find, or do. She knew where he would be. Peering into the dimly lit cellar she could see him slumped against the wall, surrounded by empty bottles and vomit, apparently unaware and uncaring of his own actions.

Supposing him to be out of the way for now she made her way along the hall towards the front door, planning to open it and call someone, anyone, for help. Just as she put a hand on the knob Sarah was grabbed roughly from behind and spun round to face her abuser. Hauling her with a force she could not find the strength to fight against he dragged her back the way she had come. With a terrible, fiendish laugh he pushed her up against the wall and it became clear to her what his intentions were. She pulled away as hard as she was able but he stopped her again by the cellar door.

Knowing what he intended to do and, even more unbearable that, even in his present state, he could see the thought of it happening in Father's cellar would quite literally be adding insult to injury, sheer terror set in as she felt herself shaking and helpless in his grasp.

It was then that Sarah found herself looking directly into the eyes of this excuse for a man who had robbed her of so much, not just the security her father had left but of love, happiness, her youthful innocence, and now her dear mother! Tears rolled uncontrollably down her face as she thought of how much they had both suffered at the hands of this ... this monster. She despised him so much she could bear to look at him no more. Suddenly all the hate and fury she felt for this man erupted in one huge rush of strength enabling her to push him with such force that, in his drunken stupor, he fell backwards through the open cellar door and down the steps. Sarah was aware of his head cracking against the bottom step as he landed sprawled out at amongst the mess at the bottom.

Sarah slammed the door. She saw the bolt drop….. She walked away.

Chapter Twenty-Nine.

What Next?

Sarah sat with her mother's lifeless body once more, not knowing what to do next. It was obvious there was nothing to be done to help her mother now but for quite some time she could not bring herself to leave. She realised she must consider her plight with great care. After all, if Sheppard was dead she could be accused of murder. If not was there a chance he may come to and come after her? On the other hand of course Sarah knew that, unless someone opened it from outside, perhaps 'the door' would protect her from this at least, and if she was not there then there would be no one to open it!

Either way, she knew deep in her heart that what she needed most now was the care and protection only John could offer her. But just what she would say to him she had no idea. Sarah kissed her mother once more on the forehead, picked up her bags and left the house. By now it was quite dark outside and there was no one about to see her go.

By the time she arrived at the Lawes house Sarah was quite distraught. Mrs Betts was shocked to see the state she was in and immediately took her into the kitchen to sit in the warmth of the range. After producing a small glass of brandy which she insisted Sarah took a few sips of to calm her down, and reassuring her that there was no one else at home until much later, Sarah was coaxed into pouring out all that had happened that evening.

After much careful consideration Mrs Betts decided what was to be done,

"As you rightly say, I'm so sorry but there is nothing we can do for poor Kate now, and she would most certainly not want to see you in such trouble over whatever has become of that awful man. We need to get you safely away with Mr Lawes before anyone finds them."

As she continued she took a comforting hold of Sarah's hand and gave it a gentle squeeze,

"You must try to get what sleep you can here tonight. Mr Lawes will be late in, but in the morning he is planning an early start for you both. Either later tomorrow or early the following morning I will call on you mother, as the neighbours are accustom to seeing me doing from time to time. When I get no answer from the door I will call on Bill and May to ask if they know where your mother is. They're bound to say no, in which case we'll call the police to report our concerns. By then you will have sailed and no one will know you were there when this happened."

Sarah thought for a minute before saying with tears in her eyes,

"But what about mother? I can't just go, I need to be here to arrange a funeral for her?"

Mrs Betts reassured her that, as a close friend of Kate's it would be a privilege to undertake such a task in a befitting manner. On that note, and with reluctance finishing off the brandy in her glass, Sarah found herself tucked up in bed in the guest room where she spent a very restless night until awoken by Mrs Betts early the next morning. After a breakfast which she felt barely able to face it was time to leave. As for John, he assumed her rather quiet, sad demeanour was due to leaving her mother. In fact he said as much to Mrs Betts and asked if she thought he should take Sarah back to see Kate before setting off.

"Certainly not," she assured him, "that will only upset her more Sir, and she has already said goodbye, so best to just give her time to deal with it in her own way. I'm sure she'll be fine given a little time."

Within the hour Sarah had said a particularly tearful farewell to Mrs Betts and Birmingham. The journey to Southampton was a long and tiring one, but at the end of it Sarah bid farewell to the shores of England forever.

Twenty-four hours into the journey John and Sarah were called to the captain's office where the news of her mother's murder and step-father's death was broken to them. Sarah had been in dread of this moment, one she knew she must face somehow. Mrs Betts had told her that she must remember that when the news came she must act shocked and upset by it, and now was that moment. Somehow she had managed to appear ignorant of what had happened up until now, but now at last she was free to give vent to all the emotion that had been building up inside her since that awful day.

John thanked the captain for his discretion in dealing with the situation, then led Sarah by the hand out of the room and back to her cabin. She could hold back her tears no more, at last she could open the flood gates which had been holding them in for so long and grieve freely for her mother; no more pretence was needed. A more pitiful sight John had never seen and one which caused him, without thought, to step forward and take her in his arms. Almost immediately he realised what he had done, and, believing he may have overstepped the mark, stepped back from her,

"So sorry Sarah, I should not have done that," he said.

And just as immediately Sarah found herself replying,

"No, please don't apologise John. Please hold me, don't let go, please don't ever let go."

From this moment on she knew he did love her, and would care for her, and she knew too that, she loved him with all her heart. She also knew that given a little time she would be able to be all that he would want her to be, and that her love for him would overcome all that had gone before in her life. He too now knew a deeper love for her than he had ever felt for any other in his life. He was well aware that he would need to be patient and not ask too much of her, just allow her to approach him when she felt ready, but at last he had that special person in his life he had always wanted.

Two weeks into their journey, and after Sarah giving her assurance that she felt she was ready and able to do so, the captain was pleased to perform their wedding ceremony. Amongst the clothes Mother had packed for her Sarah found a dress Kate had made especially for the occasion. Sarah had been unaware of this until now and, though it brought tears to her eyes to be reminded of that awful day, in a strange way it also gave her some comfort in the idea that she still could think her mother was with her in spirit. That closeness they had shared was not dead and never would be.

Though a quiet affair their fellow passengers gathered together to make this a pleasant and memorable event for the couple so that, having boarded as Mr John Lawes and Miss Sarah Burgess, they disembarked at Cape Town as Mr and Mrs John Lawes.

The following week in the Cape Telegraph there was an announcement stating that:-

Mr. John Lawes is proud to announce his marriage to Miss Sarah
Burgess daughter of the late Mr. Thomas Burgess which took place on
board ship on the occasion of her 21st birthday.

Meanwhile a week after Sarah and John left, the Birmingham Post had carried headlines which read:

Three Bodies Found

Police suspect drunken man killed his wife before falling down steps into the cellar and fracturing his head. It seems that Mr Jack Sheppard was later unable to get out of cellar when the door locked accidentally from the outside, and was consequently found dead at the top of the steps. The police also found the remains of a young man, thought now to be that of one Samuel Hackett, probably also killed by Sheppard at an earlier date. The daughter of the late Mrs Sheppard, who is now residing in South Africa, has been informed.

Chapter Thirty.

Back to Cape Town.

Sarah watched as her daughter sat with this story going round in her head and these newspaper cuttings in her hands in stunned silence, with an expression of something between amazement and sheer horror on her face. For so long Sarah had kept the doors to her memories closed, but now she had finally opened them, had this really been the right thing to do?

"Oh my dear, I'm so, so sorry, I shouldn't have burdened you with all that. Why didn't I keep quiet as I've done for so long, why weaken now when your life is so full of happiness, I had no right to spoil it for you. I'm so very sorry Lizzie."

For just an instant Lizzie sat motionless and silent, but seconds later the tears which began to trickle down her cheeks seemed to bring her back to reality, and before Sarah could utter another word she found herself enveloped in her daughter's arms. For some minutes the two women clung together, each in an attempt to console the other. Eventually, as they released their hold to wipe away their tears, it was Lizzie who was the first to speak,

"I always knew you had some dark secret hidden away Mother, but I really never expected to hear something like that. That was awful, you must have gone through hell and been so scared, and yet you've shut all of it away in your head all this time. Did Father know about it?"

"Well, no, at least I'm not totally sure how much he did know really. He never asked about it, though I believe he had some idea, but think he thought it best not to upset me by asking. He obviously knew I was upset when we left, but I think he assumed it was just because of me leaving Mother. And then when we were told about her death, and that man's of course, he even offered to take me home. There was nothing left to go home to by then of course. Dear Mrs Betts was as good as her word and wrote to assure us that she had taken it upon herself to arrange Mother's funeral which had been attended by a number of Kate's friends. John contacted his manager in the Birmingham factory to deal with the sale of my Father's house and arrange for the money from the sale to be put into an account in my name, and we just threw ourselves into building a new life for ourselves here."

Sarah went on to tell her daughter how it had been coming here back then. The journey had proved a long and arduous one, during which Sarah and John had plenty of time to become a little accustom to spending time in one another's company. Though they had spent much time together as employer and employee, the change to husband and wife had taken some time to become accustom to. Both were rather cautious, though for different reasons of course, at the beginning.

By the time they arrived at Cape Town Sarah found herself somewhat relieved to be back on dry land at last even though the crossing had been fairly smooth.

"Even so," she told Lizzie, with a bit of a glint in her eye, "when we were on deck and it did get a little choppy it was a good reason for your father to keep his arms round me to steady me, and of course I never complained."

They had spent the first couple of weeks staying in a hotel in town giving Sarah time to acclimatise to both the heat and the environment around her. "Of course dear," she told Lizzie, "you've not been to England yet, so you cannot imagine the difference. When you do go you'll see what I mean. The temperature there can be absolutely freezing in winter, and even the summers are rarely anywhere near those you are accustomed to here."

Of course, especially during those early years, John had to spend a good amount of his time out talking to people about business but, not wanting to leave her alone, he employed a young girl to help in the house. Sarah explained to Lizzie that it was from this girl that she'd learnt so much of what life here was like.

"Her name was Janet, or at least that was what we called her as her real name was hard to say! At first I couldn't understand why she was so reluctant to talk to me. There was so much I didn't understand about this country. When I pressed her for conversation she always seemed uncomfortable and would scuttle away with such a guilty look on her face," Sarah smiled at the thought of the discomfort she caused poor Janet at first.

"You see, there was so much about this country I really had no idea about, so it seemed natural to ask her as she was the person I saw most when your Father was working. When I asked him why he thought Janet wouldn't talk with me he realised I knew nothing about the rules of segregation in this country. Of course, as Janet always did the shopping and such like, I'd only been out when he was with me. You must remember, segregation doesn't exist in England. Perhaps a bit of class distinction here and there, but on the whole anyone is free to go where they like. Just you remember that dear."

"Yes, I suppose I'll have a lot to learn when we get there," Lizzie reflected.

"Anyway, once I understood, I managed to convince Janet that I didn't agree with treating people that way, and that I really would be pleased to have someone to talk to, whatever colour their skin was! After that we spent so much time together we became close friends, even though she was employed just as a housemaid to me. With her help I soon became more at home here."

Lizzie listened with interest as her mother continued, "After a while your father took me to see a house out away from the hustle and bustle of the town, yet near enough for him to attend his business daily. I'd never seen such a beautiful house, with large airy rooms, verandas upstairs, a large kitchen and the most amazing garden. This was of course the house you were born in dear, the same one that you grew up in, and unfortunately, the one your father died in."

Lizzie thought back to those days in the old family home and smiled. "Was that Janet who was my nurse when I was small? I do remember her. What happened to her? I can't remember her being around long after I started school."

"No, you're right, unfortunately she left us at that time as her mother was ill and she needed to go back to her village and take care of her. Perhaps I might have coped better after father died if I'd had her companionship, but life never goes the way we'd like it to." Sarah heaved a sigh before forcing a smile and continuing with her story,

"Those early days were such a strange mixture for me of such a deep, almost unbearable sadness every time I thought about my mother and what had happened, and yet such an amazingly deep sense of love and wellbeing I felt just being with your father. Though, as I've explained, I don't believe he knew exactly what had happened back there, I always thought he must have suspected it was something pretty awful because of the extra special care and devotion he showed me from the start. Our relationship at first concerned me as I was worried he may have felt the age difference meant I looked at him more as a father figure. This, if you can cope with me being blunt dear, was because I felt a great difficulty when it came to any real intimacy. From what I've explained to you I'm sure you'll understand how that would be."

Lizzie most certainly could see how Mother must have felt so scared to allow anyone, even Father, that near after what she had been through.

"Anyway," Sarah explained, "I loved John so much and he had such a kind and tolerant way with him that it wasn't very long before I managed to push the bad thoughts to the back of my mind and allow myself to show him all the love he well deserved and that I really felt for him. Of course it was not so long after that that you arrived to complete our little family."

Lizzie pushed her mind back to her very early days when they were a happy family of three, living in the home she had loved so much, and the memories she still could retrieve from those days. She remembered with such affection how her father used to play out on the lawn with her, hiding behind trees or amongst the shrubs, and sometimes they would lie together at the top of the small bank and roll down it, often being told off by Mother for getting grass stains on their clothes! Still, she could never keep a straight face and would burst into laughter at their dishevelled appearance afterwards.

Both mother and daughter remembered the year, when Lizzie was about ten years old, when John had taken them on a particularly special holiday along what is called the Garden Route, along the South-Eastern coast of South Africa, to show them the full beauty of the country. Along this route he had arranged for them to leave the train to be taken by a couple of rangers for a drive out on a safari into the African bush to become acquainted with some of the wildlife, the likes of which she had ever seen.

"It was truly amazing for us both wasn't it dear, and took my mind back to the time when I had sat at home in Birmingham wondering what it would be like here. Your father had shown me pictures in his books long before he asked me to marry him, and it was those of the animals, especially the elephants and those elegant giraffes, that really captured my imagination."

Sarah couldn't help noticing the look of amusement on her daughters face. "I know this must seem funny to you now, but in England we had nothing like those animals, except in zoos, so it was my first opportunity to see such creatures in real life."

It did seem odd to Lizzie to think of a country without such creatures, much in the same way it had been for her mother to think of one with them she supposed, and in that way she really began to understand some of what she had given little thought to, about just how different her future home in 'this strange land' (as Sarah had thought so long ago), would be. But still, as her mother had, she had dear Harry to take good care of her, and felt sure it would be fine, even more so if she could persuade Mother to marry George and go with them!

Sarah continued to talk her daughter through the early year's memories which she stored away in her mind. All had been a life of increasing comfort and growing happiness.

"Your father showed me so much love and devotion, much more than I could possibly have hoped for, and this gradually made me …well, not forget, but perhaps you could say, slam a door on all that had happened back in England.
I began to feel safe and happy, all was going so well with Father's business too, not a money worry in sight as you might say, meaning that you were able to receive a good education."

At this point in her story Sarah smiled to herself and looked lovingly across the room at the photo she had on the living room wall of John Lawes. Below it was one of the two of them together taken by an obliging crew member on board ship at their wedding.

She smiled at the handsome face looking down at her, almost as if still watching over her, and then heaved a sigh. If only she could see him, speak to him, just once more, even for a brief moment. She knew this could never be, but she had longed so often to hear his voice or feel the gentle touch of his hand. The smile was replaced with a look of such sadness that Lizzie moved across the sofa and put a comforting arm around her mother. "You were obviously very happy with Father weren't you?"

"Yes dear, I was so very, very happy with your father. He was always so kind, so gentle. I think that is why I found his death so very hard to come to terms with. I really am so very sorry I had to part with you for that few months but the doctors decided that I was heading for a breakdown, and left me no choice. I really wish I'd been stronger for your sake, but I know now that had it not been for wanting to get you back I don't think I would ever have got over it."

Lizzie sat in silence holding Sarah's hand for a minute before speaking. A look of understanding gradually came over her face,

"I can now understand just why you have been so guarded against the idea of letting any other man close to you. And now you're facing the prospect of losing me too when I go back to England with Harry," Lizzie said. "I can also see, after all that happened to you, just why you were so weary of him at first, and that's why you've been keeping poor George at arm's length all this time, even though I'm pretty sure you must know him well enough by now to know you can trust him too. In fact I believe you must know them both well enough by now. You must know that

George is devoted to you and would never do anything to hurt you."

Of course she was quite right, Sarah thought to herself. After all, she knew that when it was not possible to go back, the only option left was to go forward. That was always John's philosophy, and it was his insistence of this rule that had got her through the awful events of her past. He taught her to keep pushing on and never look back, and that was just what she must do now.

Somehow at this point Sarah felt suddenly as if a huge weight had been lifted from her shoulders. She had opened those doors to all the troubles that had been hidden behind them all these years; suddenly she could see clearly the way ahead. Lizzie was right, all that was gone, her beloved John had also gone though he would always have a place in her heart, but now there was dear trustworthy and loving George, waiting to step in and take away any remaining fears she might have. Of course she could trust him and, yes, she did love him, perhaps not in the same way as John, but in a new way. At forty-five years old she could see now that she wasn't old enough to give up on the prospect of a happy life after all.

"Alright Lizzie," she said suddenly, "the answer to your original question is yes."

Lizzie looked puzzled, "Do you mean 'yes' you do trust George?"

"No, I mean yes, we *will* have a double wedding, and then George and I *will* come back to England with you! After all, somebody has to keep an eye on you," Sarah heard the words but could barely believe it was her saying them.

The tears of sorrow from earlier were now replaced by tears of joy from an incredulous Lizzie, soon matched with those of her mother.

Chapter Thirty-One.

Sarah's Return.

One warm and sunny September morning, at a little church not far from the air base where Harry and Lizzie had met, all of theirs and Sarah and George's friends gathered together to celebrate this very joyous occasion with both couples. Everyone who knew them could see how happy they all were and how close they had become. Though they didn't know why, all could feel a change appeared to have swept over Sarah in particular, a change for the better they commented amongst one another.

By Early 1946 Harry was posted back to England to be demobilised. Though he travelled on a troop ship, Lizzie, Sarah and George followed on a week later, giving him time to arrange temporary accommodation for them to share not far from his parents' house in London.

As he travelled around the capital he was somewhat shocked by the devastation that had taken place whilst he was away. The war had wreaked havoc on much of the area he had grown up in. Even so his parents were thrilled to see him return and, when he introduced them to his new wife and her family, they made them all feel so very welcome. Sarah and Harry's mother Hannah soon became close friends, whilst Ted, Harry's father, took it upon himself to take George out and about to show him what he called the 'real London'. George had briefly passed through London some years previously, on his way from his native Russia, but at that time it was very different. Then there had been no war (not since the first of course), but even so he too couldn't help being shocked by the results of the bombing that had taken place.

It wasn't very long before Harry found himself new employment as a manager of a nice little country pub in the suburbs with accommodation thrown in. Lizzie was very pleased to move that bit further away from the city, and at the same time Sarah and George were fortunate too in finding a comfortable bungalow in the same area using much of the funds from the account John had set up for her so long ago. They managed quite comfortably on the rest of this supplemented by the money George earned by turning his hand to clock and watch repairing, and occasionally by the buying and selling of the odd pieces of jewellery people would bring to him.

Early one bright morning towards the end of September that year Lizzie and Harry turned up at Sarah's house without warning. "Come on Mum," Lizzie said to her, "Put your best clothes on, we're taking you out for the day."

"Why... where to? I don't understand dear," was all she could say. It soon became clear that George was in on whatever they had planned. Somewhat perplexed by what this was about she duly got changed just as a taxi arrived to take them to the station. It wasn't until the train pulled into the station that she realised that they had brought her back to her home town of Birmingham. It seemed that a client of Harry's lived there and had offered to lend them his car for a day so that Harry could drive Sarah around her old haunts.

It was not long before they pulled up outside her old family home, Tom's home, which, though presumably modernised on the inside, had changed very little on the outside except for the colour of the door. Sarah was pleased to see that it looked well cared for by its present occupants, really admiring the bright modern curtains hanging at the windows.

Harry offered to knock to see if there was anyone in who might allow them to come in for a brief look, but Sarah said no. She was beginning to feel the dark memories of that last night there beginning to creep in and suggested they move on.

The next stop was of course the house at which she had been so happy, working for and getting to know the man who became Lizzie's father, John Lawes. The gate at the end of the drive was open and Harry decided to go through it and right up to the front door.

Here he jumped out, without waiting for Sarah's approval, and rang the doorbell. Within seconds it was answered by a rather prim but friendly looking lady who explained that this was now a retirement home of which she was the matron. Harry explained Sarah's connection to the house and Matron immediately invited them all in. She was extremely interested to hear all about the history of the Lawes family and Sarah's memories of the house, and escorted them around so that Lizzie could see her father's childhood home.

After a look around Matron took the family to the lounge for a very welcome cup of tea and sandwiches. As they sat eating these Sarah casually mentioned how her time here had been made so comfortable by the help and support of her late husband's housekeeper, Mrs Betts.

"Oh, of course," said Matron, "Mrs Betts always said she had worked here for many years. She was one of our first residents you know."

Sarah's heart jumped on hearing this. She had never expected to hear anyone speak of her dear Mrs Betts again. Matron had said she '*was*' a resident. Obviously she wouldn't be about after so long as, Sarah guessed, she would have been in her mid-sixties when they left England.

"I'm afraid I lost touch with her when my husband died as I was ill for some time after that. She was a really good friend to my mother right to the end," the end and past it Sarah thought to herself, wishing she could have returned the favour and been here to see to Mrs Betts funeral too.

"Don't worry dear," Matron assured her, "she was much loved by everyone here and when she passed away, very peacefully in her sleep I might add, we gave her a really good send off. She was just gone ninety you know!"

Suitably refreshed and reassured the family climbed back into the car for what Sarah thought must be the drive back to the station. A little way down the road Harry pulled up outside a shop and disappeared inside leaving Lizzie and her mother chatting away, oblivious to what he was doing. As he returned he opened the boot and deposited something in, but by then George had joined their conversation and off they went once more.

Secretly there was still one place Sarah's heart was telling her she longed to go to, but she had no wish to look ungrateful after all they had done for her, nor to dampen everybody's spirits. Her mind drifted to the place she was thinking of, almost leaving her in a trancelike state for a few moments until, quite suddenly, she was jolted back to reality by George opening her door and Lizzie saying, "Come on Mum, out you get."

And there in front of her was that very place she had longed to go, and there was Harry handing her a bouquet of beautiful yellow roses. This was the cemetery in which her mother was laid to rest all those years ago, arranged as promised by dear, sweet Mrs Betts!!

All four walked together around the cemetery, reading the names on the gravestones in search of the one they had come to find. "Look Mum, here it is, this is Grandma isn't it?" Lizzie was first to spot it.

Here Lies
Kate Burgess
Loving wife of Thomas
Mother of Sarah

Died 28th Oct, 1921
R.I.P

Sarah starred in sheer disbelief for a while, tears flowing freely down her cheeks, before turning to her daughter to exclaim, "She didn't use his name, dear Mrs Betts didn't call her Kate Sheppard! Look, she had my father's name put on here. What a wonderful thing to do. I wish I could have thanked her for that but she didn't tell me."

As she turned back to look again Sarah's eye was caught by the name on the stone next to her mother's, 'Mrs Phyllis Betts'. The sight of this and the feeling that Mrs Betts was still right there alongside Kate, as it were, watching over her still, left Sarah not knowing whether to smile or cry.

Lizzie took one rose from the bouquet and placed it gently on her grandmother's grave before giving her mother a warm embrace and saying, "take as long as you like Mum, we'll wander back and sit in the car.

Sarah knelt down for a minute to clear the odd bits of grass that had grown above the edges of the two graves, then stood back up. She placed a single rose on Mrs Betts stone, thanking her as she did so, then placed the rest alongside Lizzie's on her mother's grave. She wondered if the family had realised that it was exactly twenty-five years to the day that poor mother had died, and was this why they had chosen today to bring her as this was the first chance she had had to come here?

All of a sudden she fancied she could hear Mother calling, "come on, it's time to get some fresh air," as she used to call her and her father from the cellar. But now she knew somehow that this voice was telling her it was time to let the past go,

To finally close the doors on that chapter of her life and live again.

Printed in Great Britain
by Amazon

69064416R00098